SUSIE DAY

THE SECRETS OF THE SUPERGLUE SISTERS

PUFFIN

PUFFIN BOOKS

UK | USA | Canada | Ireland | Australia
India | New Zealand | South Africa

Puffin Books is part of the Penguin Random House group of companies
whose addresses can be found at global.penguinrandomhouse.com.

www.penguin.co.uk
www.puffin.co.uk
www.ladybird.co.uk

Penguin
Random House
UK

First published 2017

001

Text copyright © Susie Day, 2017
Cover artwork copyright © Lisa Horton, 2017

The moral right of the author and illustrator has been asserted

Set in 13/18pt Baskerville MT by Jouve (UK), Milton Keynes
Printed in Great Britain by Clays Ltd, St Ives plc

A CIP catalogue record for this book is available from the British Library

ISBN: 978–0–141–37537–3

All correspondence to:
Puffin Books
Penguin Random House Children's
80 Strand, London WC2R 0RL

For Fliss

Thank you for letting me borrow your egg

HOW IT ALL BEGAN

Once upon a time there were two little girls named Georgie and Jem. They were both very beautiful,

Why does your name come first?

and both very clever,

Nope.

and both very interesting.

We sound boring now - if you have to tell people you are interesting, you are probably not interesting.

Jem, I'm doing the writing because yours looks like spiders, and you have to let me be in charge of something.

I am - the writing is the bit you are in charge of. I am in charge of everything else.

1

They were both eight years old, and went to the same school, and at the end of the day Georgie was always the last one left in the playground, waiting to be collected, all by herself.

Aww.

I know.

That's sad.

A little bit, yes.

They weren't really friends until, one day, Jem was left behind in the playground at the end of the day too. She looked very upset (*I didn't*) about being left all by herself (*I wasn't*) and about her mum leaving home for ever and ever (*OK, maybe a bit*). Luckily Georgie already knew all about being a Product of Divorce, which is what you are called if your parents split up.

It isn't.

It is sometimes.

To cheer Jem up, Georgie told her a very funny joke about frogs. They became fast friends.

2

And then one day Georgie's mum kissed Jem's dad on the lips – in the middle of Parents' Evening, in front of everyone – because they had fallen in love.

You missed out a lot of things.

I did. It's called being economical.

OK, I'm telling it now because you missed out nearly all the important things.

Once upon a time there were two girls called Jem and Georgie and they were best friends because of nothing at all to do with frogs or divorces, or because they both wear glasses, even if that is what stupid Caroline says. They were just friends because they liked each other best out of everyone in the whole class. They did everything together, like handstands against the wall, and writing secret messages in backwards writing and putting them in each other's lunch boxes, and also sometimes telling frog jokes to cheer each other up when they were left behind at school because their rubbish parents had forgotten they existed.

Mum doesn't forget I exist. She just works very long hours.

Whatever.

Whenever Jem went to Georgie's house, the carpets were all really soft and deep like fur coats. There were loads of games without any pieces missing, and a big bedroom just for Georgie, and Jem always said, 'I wish I lived here all the time.'

Whenever Georgie went to Jem's flat, she really liked that as well.

I did. Your dad makes jelly and ice cream and tinned peaches for dessert. My mum says they taste of tin instead of peaches. But I think they taste of deliciousness.

Georgie always said, 'I wish we were sisters, and not just best friends.'

And then Jem's dad kissed Georgie's mum – at Parents' Evening, in front of everyone, on the lips.

See? I didn't miss out that much.

I haven't finished yet.

They had fallen in love. That meant going out on dates to eat chicken, and texting, and more kissing each other on the lips in front of people. But then tragedy struck! They had a big fight in Nando's and decided they hated each other! And everything was ruined! BUT then they magically remembered they were in love, and who pays the bill for chicken butterfly and macho peas doesn't matter when you are in love.

I don't remember that at all, Jem.

I do.

Instead of falling out of love like people do sometimes, they carried on being in it. The house with all the soft deep fur coat carpets didn't have enough room in it for everyone, so they bought a new one. All Georgie and Jem's dreams came true. They would be sisters at last, stuck together for always like superglue.

And they all lived happily ever after.

You can't say that - we haven't yet.

We will, though.

Yes. Yes, we will.

NEW YEAR'S EVE

JEM

Dear New Family Moving into Our Old Flat,

Hi! Come in! How are you today?

Well done for choosing here to live in. It is a nice flat and not at all mouldy apart from that one corner of the bathroom. Just don't move the extra bit of carpet by the window in the front room, because there may once have been an accident with me spilling a magic potion made of raspberry slushie and tea bags which I tried to fix with some scissors. Also, if you open the cupboard above the fridge, the door falls off and hits you on the head. (I have left you a box of plasters inside just in case.) Oh, and sorry about the scribbly drawing of a horse on the bedroom wall. We thought it would wash off. It didn't. Some of us were very young and forgivable at the time.

Anyway, I hope you will be very happy here! The last people who lived here (i.e. us) were – apart from the bit where my mum kissed Mr Gregorio the yoga instructor and then my parents got divorced. But I bet that won't happen to you! You might not even be married! Probably everything will be fine!

Please enjoy this plate of Jammie Dodgers. Happy New Year!

With love from Jemima Magee, aged 11¼

I did a drawing of the biscuits at the bottom of the page, like instructions, in case the new people didn't know what Jammie Dodgers were. I'm not good at drawing, though. It looked more like a pepperoni pizza. So I wrote *BISCUITS* underneath, with an arrow. And a row of kisses, because it never hurts to be friendly.

Then Dad clapped his hands together and yelled, 'Five minutes to go, lads! Five minutes to go!' and my heart went skip like it wanted to fly right out of me, all the way to the new house.

'Yesyesyes,' I said.

'Noooooo!' wailed Tilly, and lay down on her face on the kitchen floor.

'Why is Doris Morris in the bin?' shouted Noah, running in from outside. He was hugging a furry penguin.

'She's not in the bin, she's in the charity recycling,' I told him. 'You had to choose just your favourite softies to take with us – remember? Not, like, a hundred thousand million families of penguins and otters and bears with hats on.'

'I've written a poem,' said Tilly, still lying on her face.

'Doris Morris is my most favourite for ever,' said Noah firmly, and he put the penguin in his backpack.

'My poem is called *The Tragedy of Tilly Magee*,' said Tilly. 'It goes like this: *Oh woe is Tilly, alas and alack and booooo to everything . . . She will never see her one true love's face again . . . And it is such a nice face too . . . Life is plop.*'

'That doesn't rhyme,' said Noah, reappearing holding a bulgy plastic bag.

'I'm too upset for rhyming,' said Tilly.

'He's not your one true love, he's the postman,' I told her while peering into the bulgy bag. It was full of more softies: a pink bear, a mouse with one ear and a long, overstuffed snake.

'No,' I said.

'*Yes*,' said Noah, grabbing the snake and the mouse, and squishing them into his backpack too.

'I haven't done the second verse yet,' said Tilly. 'Listen: *Oh woe is me, my letter box may fill up, but my massively sadtimes heart will be for ever empty . . .*'

I decided to ignore them both because we only had less than five minutes left, and being the oldest I had my important witchy things to do.

Some people think I'm not really a witch. I only do kind things, like a happiness spell which is actually more just a hug, and magicking away holes in socks by knowing how to sew them up, but I think very witchful thoughts while I'm doing them, so it totally counts. Good witches know that when you move house, you have to say goodbye to all the rooms and the memories, or it's a bad omen. I do it every time we move.

Only this time it was extra exciting.

We used to be just the Magees.

Dad.

Mum.

Me, Jemima, though everyone calls me Jem because it's quicker and because Mum says I'm sparkly like a precious gem (on my insides, with my imaginative brain and my interesting ideas, not my outsides, which are round: round glasses and a round face and a short haircut that *some* people say is unflattering but I don't care).

Tilly – who is Matilda really – who is nine, with massive woolly black hair and, Mum says, 'the personality of a pre-emptively teenage black cloud'.

Noah, who's six and likes making all his toys be in families like the Sylvanians – only it doesn't matter if a fox and a tiger have dinosaur babies, and who, Mum says, is called Noah because you spend all day saying 'No!' and 'Argh!' at him.

Plus Spooky the black cat.

And we were brilliant at being Magees for years and years – till I was eight, which is quite old. But then Mum kissed Mr Gregorio, and Dad and Mum decided they didn't like telling jokes any more, or singing along in the car, or each other – so Mum went to live in a shiny flat in Croydon by herself, which she said she liked best.

She doesn't really. No one would want to live in a flat in Croydon, even a shiny one, all by themselves. And obviously we were all massively sad, and maybe some of us cried in the playground at the end of school once. Maybe twice. But that's divorces for you. There's a lot of shouting, and then someone has to go to Croydon. And it couldn't be Dad, because he's the only one who knows how to make macaroni cheese.

Then our dad fell in love again – with my best friend's mum, which is what everyone's dad should do because it's very convenient.

Obviously I could see it was going to be the best thing that had ever happened to us ever, because of being the oldest and knowing more things. And Dad knew too, because he is in love. Last night we stayed up really late together doing the last bits of packing, and he had two beers and made a picture of Mina's face out of fridge magnets.

'I love that woman,' he told me, pointing at her nose, which was made out of Southend Pier.

'I love new houses where you get to live with your best friend who is now your sister, nearly,' I told him.

And we giggled a lot.

But the others were too busy writing poems to the postman and hugging penguins to get properly excited.

There was a honking noise from a taxi outside.

'It's time, lads, it's time!' yelled Dad, chasing Spooky the cat round and round the kitchen so he could be poured in through the hole in the top of the kitty carrier.

'You'll like it when we get there, I promise,' I told him through the bars.

Spooky mewed crossly.

'Je-e-e-em,' said Noah.

Tilly put her hairy head on my foot. 'Je-e-e-e-e-em,' she said too.

I looked at Dad, a bit pleady.

It wasn't about the postman really, or softies in the charity bag. We weren't just moving to a new house. We were turning into a whole new family. And we'd done that once already when Mum left and it had been completely miserable.

(Maybe I cried in the playground more than twice. Maybe we all did.)

Dad rubbed his hands together. 'Ah, come on now, lads – it'll be grand when we're in. There's only the one pool full of piranha fish you have to cross on the driveway . . . Then just a wee wall of fire inside the front door . . . You'll get used to the troll we've put in behind the toilet in no time . . .'

He looked back at me, a bit pleady too, because he is best at jokes, not feelings.

So I got on the floor and pulled Tilly's socks down till she got cross enough to roll over and sit up and brush her hair out of her face. I blew on Noah's long blond hair till he wriggled.

'Superglue,' I whispered.

Superglue is like secret Magee code. One year, for Dad's birthday, all three of us bought him a present from the charity shop with our pocket money: a china giraffe with delicate spindly legs and gold paint on its hoofs. We carried it all the way home, ever so carefully – but when we wrapped it up in proper crackly paper, something went *snap*. One of the delicate spindly legs was in Noah's fist, and the rest was on the table. We all felt flat, like a popped balloon. But Mum said, 'Superglue!' and we stuck that leg back on in no time, and Dad said it was his favourite present in the history of birthdays.

So that's what *superglue* means for Magees. *Don't worry*, and *Let's make it better*. Because there's not a broken thing that can't be fixed, not anywhere.

Tilly and Noah both lifted up their heads, looking hopeful.

'Is there really a troll?' asked Noah.

'And a pool of piranhas?' asked Tilly.

'Only one way to find out,' said Dad, with his best twinkly smile.

'Come on! Hurry up!' I whispered, shooing them out as Dad gave my hand a squeeze.

I jumped into the car, and I shut my eyes and crossed my fingers and crossed my toes inside my shoes, which is a secret witchy way to make sure good things happen. (Don't tell anyone.)

GEORGIE

'Kitchen – second bedroom – top-floor bathroom,' Mum reeled off, directing the Heavenly Removals people into the new house with a flick of her wrist.

'Um. What's that smell?' I said, wrinkling up my nose as we stepped inside.

'New paint,' said Mum in a rapturous sort of voice, and sniffed deeply. 'Isn't it marvellous, Georgie?'

Then she sniffed all the walls. And the carpets, and inside the kitchen cupboards, and even the water coming out of the taps.

It *was* marvellous, probably. But I went around opening windows instead, even though it was December, because asphyxiating your new siblings didn't seem like a good start to a family.

Then I stuck up all my hand-decorated colour-coordinated name cards, so everyone would know which bedroom was theirs.

'Blu-Tack? On the new doors? I don't think so, Georgie,' said Mum, pulling them all down again.

'Can we put the Christmas tree here?' I asked, pointing at the bare, white-painted wood floorboards in a corner of the bare white living room.

All the other houses on Sorrel Street still had their decorations up: twinkling lights, and trees loaded with sparkly baubles in every window. We'd had to take all ours down for the move, but I knew where they were: in the big box marked *CHRISTMAS* in the very first removal van. It would be the perfect welcome: cosy and friendly and warm.

'Next year,' said Mum, frowning as she smiled. 'All that mess for a few days? Don't be silly, Georgie.'

I am mostly a positive person. But my shoulders went droopy at the thought of no more Christmassiness at all for a whole year.

Then Mum saw my face, and her frown went soft and crumply as she pulled me into a hug. 'Oh, darling, I'm sorry. I just—'

'You want everything to be perfect,' I whispered into her shoulder, hugging her back.

'I do. New, and special, and perfect. Like . . . like we didn't have before. You understand, don't you?'

When she pulled back, her eyes were a little bit shiny.

I nodded.

I understood *exactly*. I wanted it too.

There was a scrunch of gravel on the drive outside, and a lot of yelling.

'They're here,' breathed Mum, gripping my arms.

'They're here!' I said, running outside as they all climbed out of the taxi Mum had booked.

'You're here!' I yelled, and hugged Jem as hard as you can hug someone who is carrying an angry cat in a plastic cage.

She put down the cat so we could hug some more, and jump up and down on the scrunchy gravel.

'Apparently we're pleased to see you,' said Mum, laughing as she gave Joel a kiss. She laughed again as she wiped away her purply lipstick from his lips.

I gave Tilly and Noah a hug too, feeling a bit shy. I was definitely excited about having a brother and sister as well as a Jem. I hoped they liked me. True, the one time I put my hand out to hold Noah's while we crossed the road, he licked it, and whenever I tried to talk to Tilly she put her hair over her face – but Jem says she does that to most people. It would be different now that we were practically related.

Then I shook Joel's hand – rather stiffly, because we have agreed not to hug.

I wasn't completely sure about having a new dad. But we were only practically related, not actually related, so he wasn't one really. He was just a strange man I didn't know very well coming to live with us. It would all be fine.

Joel craned his head back, staring up at the house with his shiny face.

(He was in an accident when he was little. It makes him look a bit crinkly in places, and too smooth in others. He always says he was in a fight with a dragon, 'and you should see the dragon' – but it was a spilled kettle really.)

'Did it get bigger?' he said, laughing. 'Did you

go out shopping for a bigger house in the same place while I wasn't looking?'

'Are we rich now?' whispered Noah.

'Do we have to talk posh?' asked Tilly.

Jem squeezed my hand and shook her head. 'Don't be daft. We're still us. Just with more house. Let's find the troll!'

Before I could promise there wasn't one, she had grabbed the cat cage and sprinted inside and up the stairs, Tilly and Noah at her heels.

'Shoes off indoors, with the new carpets, hmm?' Mum called after them. 'And remember – the cat will stay in the kitchen for the first week, yes? In case of any little accidents? Like we agreed?'

Upstairs, Jem was peering uncertainly at the bedroom between Tilly's and Noah's; at the double bed and the beigey carpet.

'Not us.' I tugged her past it and turned onto another flight of stairs. 'We've got the whole top floor to ourselves – look. And this,' I said grandly, 'is *your* room.'

I'd picked it for her myself, because it has sunny yellow walls and a window seat, and I could just picture her sitting in it thinking up things for us to do. That's what being friends with Jem is like: always exciting. All the things I'm good at, you have to practise and practise and practise, and have lessons. But Jem never even tries to do things perfectly. She just does them, and when she gets bored she stops and finds something else. That's why we're best friends.

Jem just stood there, blinking. Then she turned and walked across the little square of carpet to peer into my bedroom: lavender walls, with deep blue carpet and sloping ceilings.

'I thought we'd be sharing,' she said. 'Not your room and my room. I thought we'd have bunk beds, and we could take turns on who had the top one, and tell each other stories all night instead of going to sleep, and it would be like having a sleepover all the time, always.'

'Mum decided we'd like separate rooms more,' I mumbled, feeling fluttery. Now she said it, I knew that her idea was better, and it wasn't all turning out new and special and perfect after all.

'Never mind,' said Jem, striding back into her room and jumping on the bed. 'This way you can do violin practice in the morning without it being right in my ear. And I can put my craft corner here, and all my crystals and witchy books here, and I can be messy, and you can be tidy, and actually it's best. Oh! Did you make this?'

Her door sign was on the bed where I'd left it: bright yellow, with *JEM* in stencilled gold pen writing on the front, and a picture of a lion and a bright shiny sun.

I nodded.

'I love it, it's brilliant,' she said.

And she stuck it on the door with Blu-Tack.

That night, just as I was starting to have a dream about cats who lived in Christmas trees, Jem woke me up with a flash of her phone torch in my face.

'Argh!' I said – quite reasonably, I felt, under the circumstances.

'Shh!' said Jem. 'Get up. Now. It's nearly midnight!'

I put on my dressing gown and followed her back into her bedroom.

Down below, Sorrel Street was coming back to life. Music trickled from brightly lit houses. People spilled outside, laughing and chatting: grown-ups with glasses of wine and party hats, children in pyjamas, two hairy greyish dogs from the two houses opposite ours barking loudly till they were bundled back indoors with a shout of 'Stop waking everyone up, Wuffly!' which was loud enough to wake even more people up.

'Are we going down there?' I whispered, feeling excited. Mum never bothered with New Year's Eve parties; not when it was just the two of us. I knew living with Jem would be full of adventures.

But Jem was frantically moving the phone torch under her bed.

'Have you lost something?'

'Spooky,' she whispered guiltily. 'He was lonely in the kitchen, I could tell. So I let him out so we could have cuddles on my bed. But when I woke up he was gone, and now it's nearly midnight. On New Year's Eve!'

'Is this a witchy thing?' I asked gently. 'Is he supposed to turn into a handsome prince at midnight? Or back into a pumpkin? Because . . . I think he's actually just a cat, Jem. Even if you are completely really a real witch, obviously.'

25

(To be honest, I'm not sure she is. I don't think witches exist at all. But it's not very best-friendly to say so.)

'New Year's Eve!' she said, her eyes filling with tears. 'Midnight! *Fireworks!*'

And then I understood – because the last time there were fireworks, Spooky had run away to hide in someone else's garden and they hadn't been able to find him for three whole days. And if Spooky ran away this time – from the new house; the brand-new house he didn't know was home – he might never come back.

Suddenly I felt terribly worried about all my open windows.

'We'll find him, I promise,' I said. Then I went to wake up Mum.

Jem hopped up and down with even more worry – but what Jem doesn't know is that Mum is really brilliant in a crisis. She didn't say, 'I told you he had to stay in the kitchen!' or 'Why aren't you asleep, it's the middle of the night!' She put those in a pocket for later and gave Jem a hug.

'Come on, sweetheart. There's still seven minutes to go. Finding one cat usually takes six, tops.'

26

Joel fetched torches and hunted in all the cupboards, even though he was only wearing pants. With all Jem's calls of 'Spooky! *Spoooooookyyyyyy!*' Tilly and Noah woke up too – so we all joined in the search together. We switched on the lights. We looked under every bed and behind every sofa. We searched every room with an open door, waving torchlight around the piles of still-packed boxes as the last minutes of the old year ticked away – until at last mine caught a flash of black fur and glowing eyes in the downstairs bathroom as Spooky leaped into the sink.

'Found him! Quick – help!' I yelped.

'*Ten!*' echoed down the street outside.

'Just hold onto him,' yelled Joel, running down the hallway, still in his pants. 'We need – we'll get – um . . .'

'*Nine!*'

I'd never picked Spooky up before. He felt like a very furry stream of water running through my fingers. Then he turned into something sharp with teeth and claws that didn't like me much.

'Jem!'

'Just a minute!'

'*Eight!*'

'Where do you normally put him, Jem, sweetheart? What did you do last year?'

Spooky writhed and wriggled and gnawed on my wrist as I clamped my arms around him.

'*Seven!*'

'Um, well, we made him a nest in a box in the airing cupboard, with soft things around him to muffle the noise . . .'

'*Six!*'

Outside I could hear lots of thumpy noises, and boxes being shifted around, and muttering.

'Whoa, Mina, you don't have to—'

'*Five!*'

'Hush, Joel, it's fine. There – that one next!'

'Hurry up, Daddy!'

'*Four!*'

The bathroom door was wrenched open.

Outside, in the hallway, instead of a neat stack of cardboard boxes waiting to be unpacked, there was now a sort of gigantic cardboard castle taking up the whole space. There were four walls, making a small square space inside, lined with soft and fluffy white towels. Lying discarded to one side was an empty packing box with *NEW LINENS: BATHROOM 3* written on the label in Mum's careful handwriting.

'Oh, Mummy,' I breathed, because I knew she'd spent three hours in John Lewis touching all the different towels to pick out her very favourite.

'*Three!*'

'Hurry!' wailed Jem.

I stepped forward and hurled the wriggling Spooky at the nest of new towels.

'*Two!*'

Mum jumped forward and thumped another box over the hole so he couldn't leap out.

'*One!*'

We all leaped onto the castle as little black paws appeared round the edges of the hole, scrabbling to escape.

Bong! Bong! Bong!

The echoey sound of Big Ben chiming twelve on TV filtered down the street, followed by fireworks up above. There was a lot of oohing from the street outside.

'Well done, lads,' said Joel, over the feeble sound of Spooky mewing in fear and scratching at the boxes.

'Thanks,' mumbled Jem in a sniffly voice.

'It's only towels,' said Mum in a slightly strangly voice.

'Can we go and watch the fireworks?' asked Tilly as another chorus of oohs went up outside.

They hurried into the night, making *Brr* and *Ouch* noises in bare feet on the scrunchy gravel.

'Put some clothes on, Joel – you can't meet our new neighbours like that!'

'Ah – start as you mean to go on, eh?'

Jem stayed clinging onto the castle of boxes, her face pressed against the gap where Spooky's whiskery black nose peeped out.

So I stayed too.

'Happy New Year, Georgie,' she said.

'Happy New Year, Jem,' I said.

It was my happiest New Year ever.

JANUARY

JEM

Hi Mum,

It's awful here. My yellow bedroom is like living inside a banana and it's up loads of stairs. There's one of those toilet seats that bites you on the bum. There's beigey carpet everywhere and I have already dropped purple ink on it. (It's fine. I put a vase on top. This is a very vase-y sort of house.)

The other thing is the house is completely definitely haunted by GHOSTS. They make creaking noises and open doors all by themselves, and I think one ate the last Jaffa Cake out of the secret biscuit cupboard. Though that might have been Tilly because she is a total Jaffa Cake fiend. Anyway, it's a problem.

Feel free to rescue us any time and take us to Croydon. I don't mind sleeping on the floor.

Love and kisses from Jemima Magee, aged 11¼
(and the others)

'You aren't really going to send that, are you?' asked Georgie, peering over my shoulder while I wiggled my fingers over Mina's laptop.

'Of course! I have to tell my mum we're sad and tragic, so she knows we miss her and she isn't being forgotten about because we're borrowing your mum to live with,' I explained. 'It'll cheer her up.'

Georgie looked unconvinced. (I could tell she was thinking about the inky carpet.)

Then Tilly trailed into Mina's office, dragging her longest, blackest skirt across the carpet.

'Well? What's he like?'

Tilly sighed. 'It's not even a man one! It's a woman. She doesn't have a scruffly beard at all! She's all blonde and perky-faced, and she said, *Morning, sweetie pie*, to me. It's the end of the world!'

She flopped face forward across the desk, hair hanging down towards the floor like sad clouds.

I leaned in close to Georgie. 'Wherever we move to, Tilly's always in love with the postman – or, um, postwoman.'

'Post*person*, I think,' said Georgie, thinking. 'Or postie? That works.' She pulled out a chair and sat level with Tilly's head. 'You could still be in love with the postie when it's a woman, Tilly. That's allowed.'

Tilly lifted a chunk of hair back and peered out with one eye. 'Really?'

Georgie nodded seriously.

'She did have nice eyes,' said Tilly in a wistful voice. Then she wandered off, mumbling, '*Morning, sweetie pie*,' under her breath.

'Do you think she likes me now?' whispered Georgie.

'Of course she does,' I said, because everyone should like Georgie. I sucked my lip. 'Does your mum like me?'

'Of course she does,' said Georgie, looking at her knees.

We both sat quietly for a bit having thoughts. I don't like being quiet, though.

'Let's get rid of all those ghosts.'

I went and fetched supplies from the kitchen, which were a box of matches and a jar of Mediterranean herbs. 'It's supposed to be sage, but there isn't any. It's probably mostly the same. It tells ghosts and any lingering spirits to bog off.'

'No – Jem – don't you think—?'

'Yow!'

It turned out that lighting the herbs in a little glass jar and then holding it wasn't a very good idea. I threw it in the air and licked my hot hurting hands – while Georgie told me all about convection, which is science for why glass gets hot. She really is very clever.

Then we ran around putting out the little herby fires that were now all over Mina's office floor.

When we were done, there was only one little scorch mark. We put a vase on it.

'Why does it smell like burnt chicken in here?' Dad asked, peering in. 'Wait – never mind, I don't want to know. Come and give Mina a hand with the unpacking for a wee bit longer, girls, eh?'

When you move into a massive house and squish two families together, there is nothing but unpacking for days and days, apparently. It took me about half an hour to put all my sewing projects and art things, and the magic crystals that Mum gave me on the big shelves in my yellow room. Once Noah had put all his families of softies in his bed (they took up most of it), he was finished too. Tilly built a sort of cave over her bed out of dark blue sheets and blankets, and then emptied everything she owned inside it so it looked neat. But the McKays had boxes and boxes of stuff, and every time you emptied one out, there was another one underneath.

Weird stuff too. I thought Mina's things would all be brand new and shiny, like Croydon but better, because she is an important business person and quite fancy. Some of it was: matchy cups and plates and bowls in all the cupboards, with no chips, and new sofas that had plastic wrapped round them.

But loads of Mina's stuff was really old.

There was a rocking horse with glass eyes and creepy, real-looking white hair, and brown fur that had rubbed off in places and showed a hard sort of skin underneath that made you go shivery if you touched it.

'Not a toy,' said Mina firmly as it was rolled into place on the white-painted floorboards under the big window in the front room.

There was a glass case edged with black metal, with two birds inside perching on a branch; real birds, stuffed, and a nest with pale speckly eggs between them.

'Also not a toy,' said Mina, putting it on the highest bookshelf in the office.

And there was an egg all by itself too; a huge egg, as big as Noah's head, with its own round stand made of wood so it couldn't tip over.

'Ostrich egg,' said Mina proudly, placing it on the shelf over the fireplace in the back room very carefully. 'It's about a hundred years old. It belonged to my grandfather, and he gave it to me. It's not to be touched or picked up or moved because it is—'

'Not a toy,' we all said together.

'Was your grandfather an explorer, like in Victorian times?' I asked, because it was an interesting egg and I wanted it in a weird hungry way. (Not to eat. Just to have.)

But Mina and Georgie both giggled.

'I'm not that old!' said Mina. 'He worked for an auction house. Became quite a collector. You get used to being around antiques after a while . . . I think they make a house into a home, don't you?'

When she went away, we all crowded around under the egg: me, Georgie, Tilly and Noah.

'Wow,' said Noah.

'Yeah,' said Tilly. 'Wow.'

'I didn't know eggs even came that big,' said Noah.

'Or lasted a hundred years,' said Tilly.

I could tell Georgie was pleased they liked it. She had blushy pink spots on her face, and she twisted her feet on the floor. I was pleased too.

'I wonder what it would smell like if it broke,' said Noah.

Georgie went stiff.

'That is a thing we will not find out, ever,' I said, steering Noah and Tilly out of the room.

Then I fetched Dad's giraffe with the glued-on leg, and put it on the shelf beside the egg.

'Hmm,' said Georgie, her head on one side. She stroked the knobby bump of glue with one finger. Then she turned the giraffe round so you couldn't see the join. 'Much better.'

I waited till she'd moved, and then I turned it back.

Me and Georgie lay on the rug and looked at the ceiling.

'How old *is* your mum?' I asked.

'Thirty-four,' said Georgie. 'But she looks younger – everyone says.'

It was true. Mina had long brown hair with blondish streaks that always looked smooth and bouncy, like it had just been blow-dried. She wore perfume and posh trouser suits and clicky heels and deep purply lipstick for work, and white shirts with no crumples and the sort of jeans that fitted everywhere on days off. She invented Fairy Dusters, which is a cleaning company where they come round to your house in a little van with a pink fairy on the side, and wave a magic wand to make everything sparkly. Well, they do in the advert. One day I was going to tell her what real fairies are like, and she would be horrified – real ones aren't pink and wandy, they are super mean – I got a book all about them for Christmas – but not yet because I wanted her to definitely like me first. Georgie says she does already, but I think she just likes Dad, and we are sort of acceptable attachments. The only time we have ever had a whole conversation, just the two of us by ourselves, it was about school, and that was more her talking *at* me because I don't really care about school – and then she looked super relieved when her phone rang and she could go and talk to her assistant, Martin, about spreadsheets instead. So I don't think she likes me yet. But I reckon we could totally be sort of friends once we've lived in the same house for a bit. I mean, not as much as my actual mum. But comfy, like old jeans.

'How old is Joel?' asked Georgie.

'Forty-two,' I said. 'I don't think he looks younger, though.'

He doesn't. It's not his fault. He used to have lots of blond hair, long enough for a ponytail, but now he's going all bald and straggly. And there are all his scars from operations. He doesn't look young at all. But he still has a twinkly smile and bright blue eyes, and he can make you laugh till you think you might be sick.

Georgie pressed her lips together, like she was agreeing but being nice about it. Georgie's good like that.

'Mum says he's a really soft kisser, though.'

We both giggled.

We'd both seen them kiss a hundred times. They've calmed down a bit now. But people who've just got together kiss loads. Like, even while they're just making toast.

'Do you think we'll still be friends when we're as old as forty-two?' Georgie asked, moving her legs in the air like she was riding a bike.

'Course,' I said. 'We're sisters now. Superglued together for ever.' Then I scratched my nose. 'Unless you're dead by then, obviously.'

Georgie sighed, and kept cycling.

I was going to ask whether I could have the egg if she did die before she was forty-two. But I didn't bother. She was bound to say yes.

GEORGIE

It turned out there was a lot to get used to, being part of a whole new family.

Obviously it was brilliant living with Jem, and it was a little bit like we were sharing a bedroom anyway because her room was a mess of half-started bits of sewing or clothes all over the carpet, and she was fed up with it so she kept coming to lie on my bed. (My room's always neat. It's not because I'm boring. I'm not boring. I just like things to be in their right places, that's all.)

And sometimes I got woken up by a cat walking over my face, which was interesting.

Mum didn't go into the office at all over the holidays – not now there was someone at home to be kissy with – which meant baking cakes, and coffee smells, and curling up on the sofa with soppy DVDs to communally weep at.

But I still wasn't really sure if Tilly and Noah liked me. They walked out of rooms when I walked in. They whispered behind their hands. At dinner, when I sat down, they scooted their bottoms all the way along the bench to the far end of the reclaimed-pine refectory table (that's what Mum calls it; it just means it's really long) just so they didn't have to sit next to me.

'Enjoy it, kiddo,' said Joel, seeing my face fall. 'Once they start to like you, you'll never get rid of them. They'll use you like a sofa cushion.'

'They'll make pleady eyes till you give them your last square of chocolate,' said Jem.

'They'll make you play games and get narked if you don't let them win,' said Joel.

'Only don't let them win either, because they get narked about that too,' added Jem.

Tilly and Noah made snarly faces from the end of the table.

'I was the oldest in my family too,' said Mum, smiling understandingly at Jem.

I wriggled crossly in my seat. 'But – I like games. I don't mind sharing. I could be a cushion.'

I looked hopefully at Tilly and Noah – but they both hid under the table and wouldn't come out till I promised to stop.

Mum tilted her head. 'Oh, Georgie. Perhaps you need some big-sistering practice.'

On the very last day of the holidays Jem had to go off and buy all her new school uniform. Mine had been bought and packed away for months – so they went off together, Jem and Joel and Mum, and I was left behind. In charge. All by myself.

It was pretty exciting. First I made a list of *Fun Activities* like a timetable, because I like planning. Then I sat Tilly and Noah down after breakfast.

'Children,' I said in my best teacher voice. 'You can have my complete and total attention all day, because that's what big sisters do.'

'Is it?' said Tilly, glaring suspiciously at me from under her hair.

'Are you sure?' said Noah, clutching Horace Morris the brontosaurus extra tightly.

'It's what this big sister does for today, anyway. Now, first off: I thought you should both try out some musical instruments.'

They whispered behind their hands.

'We wanted to ask you if we could,' said Tilly. 'The minute we moved in. But we thought you might be scary.'

'Oh,' I said. I didn't think I'd ever been scary in my life. But it's hard to know what you're like from the outside.

'Have you got a tuba?' asked Noah.

'No.'

'Trombone?'

'No.'

'Saxophone?'

'I think you know what instruments I play, don't you?'

They both looked blankly back at me – till I took them to the study and pointed firmly at the piano and my violin case.

'Ohhhh,' said Noah.

Tilly only wanted to play the black notes on the piano – 'They seem more *me*,' she said – which made it hard to teach her a whole tune.

Noah liked plucking the violin strings as if it was a guitar – but he didn't like it at all when I tried to make him hold it properly under his chin.

'Help, Horace, she's breaking my arms!' he yelled eventually, and ran off to put his head under a cushion.

Eventually I gave up and made them orange squash and biscuits in the kitchen.

'What's next?' asked Noah, swinging his legs.

'Dancing,' I said.

At Dance Magic I do ballet and contemporary and modern, and I used to do tap, but I grew out of the shoes – and anyway, everyone in that class is about seven and quite annoying. I tried showing them some steps – but they were mostly interested in trying on my leotards and my soft-sole dance shoes and then doing a lot of handstands.

'Hairdos?' asked Tilly, fingering the hairbands and bobbles and pins on my dressing table. 'Do pretend big sisters do hairdos?'

I didn't see why not. Tilly wanted plaits like mine, and was very cross when they came out fat and stiff instead of swingy. Noah sobbed when I combed all the knots out of his long blond curls, and sniffled all the way through me weaving them into two tight French plaits (though he couldn't stop staring at himself in the mirror afterwards, whispering, 'Knobbly,' as he ran his hands over his head).

After sandwiches for lunch, I told them we were going for a walk to Queen's Park, which is a nice green space with families walking their dogs, and a duck pond.

'Why, though?' asked Noah.

'Because going for a walk is good for you,' I explained, zipping his coat right up to his chin.

'We don't usually do things that are good for us,' said Tilly doubtfully. 'Usually we do the opposite of things that are good for us.'

'It'll make a nice change, then,' I said, and put on my new white Christmas hat, which was like the face of a polar bear.

It didn't *feel* very good for us. It was the kind of freezing cold that makes your cheeks go numb and your nose go bright red. Tilly was wearing her very long black skirt, and she trailed it along the frosty grass, and then grumbled when it got damp. Noah chased all the ducks, which flapped and made the other children cry, and an old woman shouted, 'Where's your mother, young man!' very crossly.

'She's in Croydon!' Tilly shouted back, which didn't help.

'Can we play football?' asked Noah when I had steered them away from the ducks.

But I hadn't brought a ball and, when Tilly grabbed Horace Morris and kicked him off in a high arc which ended in a sad-looking twiggy bush, there were more tears.

We walked home incredibly slowly, with me dragging them both. Even though my timetable still had *Fun with Potato Printing* and *Educational Board Games* written on it, I put them in the back room with the TV remote control and a whole packet of custard creams. Then I lay on the blue sofa with cold sliced cucumbers on my eyes like Mum does sometimes, and Spooky curled up by my feet.

'Did everyone make it out alive?' called Joel as the front door banged open and closed.

'She's not being a cushion!' said Jem, sounding relieved.

Mum peeped under one cucumber slice. 'Pooped?'

'Pooped,' I whispered back.

'How are you, little ones? What have you been up to?'

Tilly and Noah were sitting at opposite ends of the other sofa, which was green leather with knobbly buttons on. They looked awful. Tilly's skirt was still damp and muddy, and she had biscuit crumbs in her wonky plaits. Noah had a plaster on his chin and was still wearing one of my pale blue leotards, all baggy, over his jeans and jumper. It was as if they hadn't been looked after at all.

'I didn't quite finish doing all the things I planned,' I started anxiously.

But Noah sat up and wriggled his shoulders happily. 'I played the violin. And we went to the park to scare the ducks.'

Tilly sat up too. 'I danced. And pianoed. And Georgie performed a heroic brontosaurus rescue in a bush.'

'Oh! Aren't you lucky,' said Mum. She leaned down to give me a kiss. 'I think you're a hit, darling.'

She gave me a big proud smile and went off to help Joel with all their shopping bags.

50

Tilly and Noah whispered ominously on the sofa. Then they hopped off it and shuffled awkwardly over to me, Noah pulling up his droopy leotard.

'Thank you for all the complete-and-total-attention fun-day things,' said Tilly.

'We saved you a biscuit,' said Noah, holding out the crumply remains of the packet, with one last custard cream left.

I felt a warm big-sisterly glow all through me as I took it.

'We did lick it,' added Noah. 'But only on one side.'

Then they shuffled off upstairs, arguing about which one of them was best at instruments.

Jem flopped onto the sofa, lying half on top of me.

'Sorry,' I mumbled. 'Do you mind? That they like me, I mean?'

'Pffrt,' said Jem. 'I've already been big-sistering for eleven years. It is *totally* someone else's turn.'

And she cheerfully ate my cucumber slices.

JEM

Dear Ghosts,

   I'm really sorry about shooing you out of the house with Mediterranean herbs. I mean, technically you have been here longer, so it's a bit rude and it isn't like I gave you time to pack or one of those notices that tell you you've only got seven days left before a man comes and takes the telly away. Only I think Mina probably brought some new ghosts with her, because creepy old weird stuff tends to have spirits attached to it. Like, I bet that rocking horse probably comes with the ghost of a small child from long long ago, with a lacy collar and velvet pantaloons and a heavy fringe. Those stuffed-bird things probably have ghosts. Even the egg. She basically brought a whole ghost ostrich into your house without a care in the world. So I was doing you a favour really.

Anyway, if you are a nice ghost who just hangs out in cupboards and doesn't bother anyone, you can come back. I made you a tiny doorway out of the Crunchy Nut Cornflakes box and put it by the window so you can see where to come in. Or you could just come down the chimney or something. Watch out for vases.

Love from Jemima Magee, aged 11¼

'Big day today, lads,' said Dad at breakfast. 'How are we doing? Jumpy tummies? Twitchy bums? Nervy collywobbles?'

It was all our first days at new school: me and Georgie at Kensal Rise Academy; Tilly and Noah at Orchid Lane Primary. Even Dad was starting a new job – as a security guard at Tesco, catching robbers with baguettes shoved up their jumpers (that's what he said). He looked very smart: proper trousers, not jogging bottoms, and a shirt with a name badge, and a hat with a peak. Tilly and Noah had red jumpers and grey trousers. I was in a scratchy white blouse with a stripy tie, and a navy blue skirt which had elastic round the waist instead of a zip. Mina picked it out when we went shopping. She said, 'I think this might be best, don't you?' while scrunching up her face nervously as if I might cry.

I wanted the short one or the one with pleats, because I like pleats, and because Georgie has the one with pleats. I think you should just choose clothes because you like them, not because they hide what you look like. They don't really hide what you look like anyway. I am still quite round, even with an elasticated waist. Mina is quite round too, even in posh trousers and clicky heels. But I'm trying to make sure Mina definitely likes me, and I wouldn't ever choose to wear boring plain white scratchy shirts and navy skirts anyway, so I just said yes.

'Can I take Doris Morris?' asked Noah.

'No,' said everyone.

'Then, yes, I have all the nervy collywobbles,' he said sadly.

'Tilly will be there to look after you,' said Mina. 'Right, Tilly?'

There was a rattling sound by the front door, and Tilly bolted. She came back clutching a handful of post, all dazed and smiley.

'*Hello again, honeybunch*,' she murmured, sinking back into her chair.

'I don't get nervous,' I said, eating my buttery toast.

I was doing a spell to create Conditions for a Good and Fortuitous Day. It worked by me eating all round the edge of my toast *widdershins*, which means going anti-clockwise (it's in my book), and then eating the middle. Spells don't have to be all magic words or potions. Real witchiness is just *in* you.

Georgie didn't say anything. She just stirred her porridge round and round without eating it.

'I'll be there to look after you too,' I said, nudging her chair leg with my foot. 'But I bet I won't have to, because everyone'll like you.'

She sucked on her spoon thoughtfully. 'I hope not *everyone*. I don't have time for that.'

The thing with Georgie is, you have to try a bit to get to know her. With me, it is obvious why I'm good to be friends with. But Georgie sort of quietly watches people, and listens and works them out, and *then* decides if they're worth the bother. That's why she always only has some friends, not lots of friends.

It means it's extra-special, me being her best one. I'm glad she picked me.

Kensal Rise Academy turned out to be much bigger than our old school, with iron gates, and a million shouty kids in the playground.

'Let's go in,' I said confidently. 'I bet we have the best teacher – they're bound to give us the best teacher if we're new.'

Georgie followed behind me, twisting the ends of her jumper sleeves into anxious knots around her fingers.

We were in 7E, and we did not have the best teacher. We had Mr Miller, who was rubbish. He was only a bit old, but he had a cardigan with leathery elbow patches, and a funny little beard like a junior wizard.

'I'm supposed to welcome you back, Seven E,' he said, lounging in his desk chair like he wanted to still be in bed. 'But we all know coming back to school after the holidays is a nightmare. Especially in January. It's always dark. It's going to be freezing cold for ages. It's probably going to rain a lot. I can only apologize. Talk amongst yourselves, why don't you. There'll be a bell in a bit.' Then he put his face on his desk and shut his eyes.

'Um. Sir?' I said, putting my hand up. 'We're new. I think you're supposed to do something. Like introduce us to the class.'

Me and Georgie were still standing by the door, wondering where to sit.

Mr Miller lifted his head off the desk and cracked one eye open.

'Never mind, sir, I can do it,' I said. 'You go back to sleep.'

Everyone in 7E giggled, so I knew it was already going well.

'Hello! I'm Jem. This is my sister Georgie. She didn't use to be my sister, which is why my last name is Magee and hers is McKay. We were supposed to start here last term but our new house wasn't ready yet. But now we live in Sorrel Street.'

'Ooh! I saw you move in! And your dad in his pants!' A girl with floppy short brown hair and freckles sat up. 'We live there too, right opposite you. Me and my brother.' She pointed at a boy – also freckly and floppy-haired – sitting two rows away. 'I'm Sam. He's called Sam too. We're twins. Yes, our mums are weirdos. Billie lives on Sorrel Street as well.'

A girl sitting right up the front gave us a big bright smile. She had dark brown skin and loads of curly hair pushed back off her face with a shiny gold band. 'Hi. I live above The Splendide. It's a café.'

'I don't know it. We only moved in on New Year's Eve so we haven't explored much yet. We will, though. I like cafés. We both do.'

'Does the other one talk?' It was a boy at the back with his feet up on the desk, tipping his chair back.

'Shut up, Alfie,' snapped the girl Sam.

'Come here and make me, sexy face,' said Alfie, tipping his chair forward and wiggling his tongue at her.

'Ew, gross,' said Sam. 'Anyway, she might have a disability or something. She's new – you don't know.'

I looked at Georgie – but she had a stiff look of terror on her face, as if she'd been locked in a freezer and hadn't had time to defrost.

'She does talk. When she thinks there are people around worth talking to.'

There was a chorus of appreciative *Ooooooohs* and *Buuuuurns* around the room.

'Oh, all right, that's enough of that,' said Mr Miller, half lifting his head. 'Welcome to our humble classroom. Find yourselves a seat, girls.'

There was only one empty chair: in the back row, next to Alfie.

I walked straight up to him. 'We need to sit here. Together. You have to move.'

His mouth fell open. Then he slowly stood up and backed away like magic.

'Wow,' said Sam. 'How did you do that?'

'I'm a witch,' I explained as we both sat down. 'I can make things happen.'

'Double wow,' said Sam, her eyes wide and impressed. Actually, everyone was impressed.

Except for me. I knew that spell with the toast-eating would work.

*

The rest of the day went just as brilliantly.

At lunch time we ate packed lunches at a picnic table with Billie, the girl Sam, and a tiny shy Nigerian girl called Efe, who whispered.

'Our friend Ruby used to sit here, but she left,' explained Billie.

'She was a strange person,' whispered Efe into her lunch box.

'So we totally have room for a new friend. Um, I mean, *two* new friends,' said Sam, coughing as if someone had kicked her under the table.

It was a bit of a squash, but Georgie squeezed in beside me, and I talked lots so they wouldn't mind that she didn't.

And at the end of the day we walked home with Billie and the twins. When we got to the row of shops at the far end of Sorrel Street, by all the bus stops and bins, Billie stopped outside a little café with red-and-white-checked tablecloths: The Splendide. She jingled her keys in her hand, but she didn't go in.

'Are you really a witch?' she asked, looking me up and down with narrowed eyes. 'Like, have you got a broom and a cauldron and stuff?'

I sighed. 'That's just stereotyping.'

'Duh,' said the boy Sam.

Billie and Sam both gave him a stare, and he wobbled off on his bike, alarmed.

'You *have* got a cauldron,' said Georgie, nudging my arm, which was a bit annoying, to be honest.

'Only a little plastic one,' I said quickly. 'I use it to keep gel pens in – that's not very witchy.'

Sam sucked on her bottom lip. 'Do you ever do magic for other people? Like – for money? Or for KitKats? Because I haven't really got any money but we always have KitKats.'

I explained about how magic only works if it's powered by sincere personal feelings or acts that bring good to the universal balance of stuff – because of being a good sort of witch. But I said I could probably have a go anyway.

'No refunds, though,' I said, because it is hard to refund a KitKat.

'Fair dos,' Sam said, and wheeled away on her bike too.

When we got home, I made footprints in the frost on the grass to spell out *JEMIMA*. It really said *JEMIMA . . .* because I forgot about jumping

61

away at the end. But Georgie said it was poetic, as if I was a work in progress, at the beginning of something exciting.

'Do you think they liked us?' she asked, hopping about to spell out her name (over in the corner, because I did mine really big). 'At school? Do you think they liked both of us?'

'Course,' I said. 'They walked home with us, didn't they? You don't do that with people you don't like – you hide in the playground till they've gone and then tiptoe behind them like a spy. We'll be invited round to their houses any minute because we're new and interesting. Then we'll practically be besties.'

I didn't really mean it, though. I already have a best friend.

GEORGIE

'Well, there's not enough coffee on the planet for the day I've had,' said Mum that night, yawning while Joel served out dinner. 'And I need to put in a call to the US at eight – don't let me forget. How did we all manage?'

'Are we having wool for tea?' asked Noah, poking his bowl.

'It's courgetti,' said Mum. 'It's just like spaghetti, only made from courgettes. It's delicious.'

'Is it, though?' asked Tilly, licking a bit.

Mum always goes on a diet in January. And another one in February, to make up for finishing off the Christmas chocolate in between Ryvitas.

'I had a cracking first day, lads,' said Joel. 'I chased a villain with a microwave oven tucked up his T-shirt all the way out of the shop, and then I commandeered a wee girl's skateboard and skidded all across the car park and then jumped on his back and shouted, *You are under arrest!* Till he cried and gave it up.'

'Really?' asked Noah.

'No. I mostly watched training videos. It was pretty boring. But tomorrow I'm catching microwave thieves – just you wait.'

Nothing dramatic had happened at Tilly and Noah's first day. Tilly had avoided talking to any new humans at all by telling everyone she was on a sponsored silence for sad children, via a cardboard sign dangling round her neck. It was still there, under her jumper.

'You do realize you'll have to talk to the rest of your class at some point?' said Jem.

'They might be nice,' I said. 'You might make friends.'

Tilly shook her hair. 'Nah. Tomorrow I'll just change the sign so I'm raising money for poorly puppies. No one can disagree with poorly puppies.'

Noah had made six friends but couldn't remember any of their names, so we thought maybe he hadn't.

'How was it, Georgie?' asked Mum gently. 'Your first day?'

Jem shot me a sympathetic look. Mum thinks I'm not very good at trying new, unfamiliar things. Which I'm not, to be honest. But her being all motherish about it doesn't make me feel any better.

'Fine, Mum,' I told her, feeling my face go hot.

'Our class is massive,' said Jem. 'We've made three best friends already, called Billie and Sam and Efe. And there's a girl called Nishat who has plaits exactly like Georgie's. And a girl called Ariadne Ocean Dupree. She's French. She doesn't speak any English at all – I asked her where the toilets were and she shrugged and said, '*Bof!*' And there's a funny jokey boy who everyone likes called Big Mohammad. I don't know if there's a Small Mohammad. And a boy called Halid, who only has one hand – we didn't stare. And a weedy boy called Edmond Hudson – everyone calls him Ed*mond* – who carries a satchel like he is from the past and has his top button done up and looks a bit like a milk bottle.'

I nudged her. 'Don't be mean.'

'I'm not! He does. A milk bottle with curly hair. Anyway, obviously we were the most interesting people there because we're new. Everyone loves new people.'

'You're missing out the most important bit!' I said, nudging her again. 'There's going to be a play. All the Year Seven classes are doing a part of it – at a big Easter Extravaganza at the end of term.'

Our new English teacher had spent the whole lesson telling us about it. Her name was Miss Eagle. She had glasses that curved up at the ends like cats' eyes, shiny brown hair in two buns on the side of her head, and a pretty wintry dress with skiers on the sticky-out skirt and a furry white collar. My last English teacher was called Mr Jeffs, and he always gave me lots of ticks, and nice comments like *Thank you for this thoughtful work, Georgina*, and *Your writing is always a pleasure to read, Georgina*, and even though usually I hate it when people call me Georgina, I liked it when it was him. But I had a feeling I was going to like Miss Eagle even more.

Jem scrunched up her face. 'How is *that* the most important bit?'

'It's *A Midsummer Night's Dream*!'

'Oh!' said Mum, smiling brightly. 'We went to see it in Regent's Park the summer before last, didn't we, Georgie? It's Shakespeare, Jem. A lovely play. You'd like it – it's got lots of magic in it.'

I nodded. 'Lots. King Oberon sends his friend Puck to put a love spell on Queen Titania so that she'll fall in love with whoever she sees next. And she falls in love with a man called Bottom who has been turned into a donkey head.'

Joel screwed up his face. 'This is Shakespeare? The *famous* Shakespeare?'

I could see what he meant. It didn't sound very much like important literature for grown-ups.

'It's meant to be funny.'

'Hmph,' said Jem. 'Maybe I'll just do costumes.' Then she muttered, 'Anyway, that's not even how love spells work.'

Then the phone rang: Jem's mum, Bridget, to ask how their first days at school had gone, and to tell Jem off for sending emails about being bitten on the bottom by a toilet seat.

While they talked, I went into Mum's office and ran my fingers along the spines of all the books until I found it: *The Complete Shakespeare*.

It was like a book from Hogwarts: huge and heavy, with a knobby brown leather spine and delicate tissue-like paper with tiny print. I flicked through until I found the right play and ran my finger down the character names.

There was a Duke and his Queen, and four silly lovers, and Titania and Oberon, King and Queen of the Fairies – but I cared most about Puck, and Moth, Peaseblossom, Cobweb and Mustardseed. In the play we saw in the park they were all dancers, in skin-tight pastel bodysuits woven about with trailing shimmery gauzy strips of fabric like wings, dotted with flowers and leaves. They weren't the main characters, although Puck had the very last speech in the play. But they were the ones I remembered best. I'd come home and tried to copy their dance, practising it in my bedroom over and over.

'How exciting!' said Mum, peeking over my shoulder. 'I'm so pleased, darling. I knew sending you to Dance Magic would be good for you. You've always been such a shy little thing. And here you are planning to be up on a stage, performing in front of the whole school!'

She clapped her hands and twirled away.

I shut the book with a snap, feeling perfectly sick.

'Ugh. Mums,' said Jem, flopping onto the armchair beside me with a heavy sigh.

'Mums,' I said sadly.

Jem took the book and glared at it. 'You don't have to be in a stupid play about bottoms if you don't want to.'

'That's just it: I *do* want to,' I said quietly.

I did, I really did. I wanted to be exactly the sort of person who goes on stage and dances in a beautiful costume, to rapturous applause. Someone brave. Someone like Mum, or Jem. Not like shy little me.

Jem sucked on her bottom lip, looking very serious. 'Don't worry, I'll help. We can fix it. 'Cos there's nothing that can't be fixed. Like superglue.'

She went to fetch Spooky and plopped him onto my lap like a warm, breathing cushion. I stroked him under his chin and behind his ears, just how he liked. He purred, long and low, his heart beating against my chest. He yawned, turning to look up at my face as if he knew I was upset. Then he bit me, hopped lightly onto the floor and padded off with his tail waving.

'Ugh. Cats,' said Jem, sighing again.

And she hugged me instead, which was probably what I'd wanted all along.

JEM

Dear Dad,

   You should probably put a lock on the upstairs bathroom door because Georgie sort of walked in on you in the shower and saw your rude parts. (She says she didn't, but she went very red so I think she was just trying to be polite.)

   Also the new secret biscuit cupboard is a bit too secret - no one has put any more biscuits in it. It is the one by the dishwasher. No Jaffa Cakes, please.

   By the way, you probably shouldn't move the vase that is now next to the blue sofa. Spooky definitely didn't scratch any holes in the blue stuff till white fluff came out. But if he had, I expect that vase would cover it up.

Love from Jemima Magee, aged 11¼

The rest of our first week at school was very strange.

First, someone stuck a *YEAR 7 RATINGS* list up on the wall in the playground, with marks out of ten for all the boys.

> Alfie Maddox: 5/10, cute but a bit up himself
>
> Big Mohammad: 8/10, good sense of humour
>
> Edmond Hudson: −22, ha ha ha ha

'*Tiens!*' said Ariadne Ocean Dupree.

'I am not,' said Alfie.

'What, cute?' said Halid.

Alfie gave him a thump.

The next day there was one for the girls too.

> Madison Hodge: 6/10, pretty but wears too much make-up
>
> Nishat Ali: 8/10, really shiny hair
>
> That new girl: 0/10, weird glasses, fat

'*Sacre bleu!*' said Ariadne Ocean Dupree.

'They might mean either of us,' said Georgie unhappily.

They didn't. We both knew they didn't. My glasses are a bit weird – that's why I like them. And I mostly don't mind the word *fat* if I say it about myself, because it is just describing, not judging, and I am a bit, and that is OK. But it's not the same if someone else says it, not at all. Not when they put it up on a wall just to be mean.

'Either way, it's awful,' said Billie, who had a 9/10 and looked both embarrassed and pleased at the same time.

After that Efe – four out of ten – locked herself in the toilets and wouldn't come out at all, even when I pretended to be a tiny vole drowning in the sink that needed rescuing. It was a really good vole impression too.

Then the packed lunches started disappearing.

'Where's my apple?' said Sam on Tuesday. 'I definitely had an apple.'

On Wednesday Georgie's lunch had a bag of crisps – but mine was missing.

'Maybe Mum thinks you don't like crisps,' said

73

Georgie, guiltily emptying some of her packet into my lunch box.

But on Thursday Billie's cheese pastry twist had a large tooth-shaped bite taken out of it.

'Unacceptable,' she said, dropping it into the bin. 'We have a lunch-box thief!'

Then, that afternoon, we had English with Miss Eagle again.

'Welcome, welcome, Seven E. How lovely to see you again!' she said.

She was wearing another sticky-out skirt, this time all silver and crinkly, and a fitted red velvet jacket that looked like rose petals. Her hair was up in a swingy ponytail with little jewels in, like dewdrops. I thought it was a bit much for a teacher really – mostly because I would like a red velvet jacket that looks like rose petals and I haven't got one.

'Sit, sit, quickly!' she said, flicking off the lights and switching on the smartboard as we sat down. 'Now, *A Midsummer Night's Dream*! I know Georgie here is the only one who's seen it, so here's a little taste . . .'

She played us a bit of film like a trailer for a movie, only with actors on a stage wearing thick white make-up, and scenery made out of big sticks, and spooky lighting. There was a woman dressed up like the White Witch from Narnia, floating in on a sheet like a cloud; there were people having a pillow fight in just their underwear (everyone giggled); there was a clown with a magic flower, and a man wearing a whole door as an outfit. All the words they said sounded weird – like poetry, kind of, and not quite in English.

'Was it like this when you saw it?' I whispered to Georgie.

'Sort of,' she whispered back, her eyes wide and shiny.

I thought it was rubbish, unless you liked big sticks and clowns and stuff.

'Are we doing it just like in the film, miss?' asked Big Mohammad.

'I'm not doing a pillow fight in my pants, miss,' said Halid.

'You can't ask us to do anything in our pants, miss,' said Madison.

Lianne hit her with a copy of *War Poems for Schools*.

'Yes, thank you,' said Miss Eagle, taking the book and turning all the lights back on. 'We won't be doing it quite like that – that's the wonderful thing about Shakespeare: it's endlessly adaptable. And we'll be doing a slightly shorter version of the text at the Easter Extravaganza – so much to fit in! But before I decide which class gets which scene, we need to hold a little audition. Very relaxed! No pressure!'

It was too late. I could feel Georgie go stiff with not-relaxed pressury feelings at once. It was going to be like our Year Six Christmas play at Begbrooke Primary all over again. I'd have to push her onto the stage, and then stand behind her shouting all her lines while she moved her mouth up and down like a ventriloquist's dummy.

But it was much worse than that.

'You'll be great,' I whispered, squeezing her hand. 'You already know what the play's like; you'll be better than everyone.'

But before it was Georgie's turn, Halid took the book Miss Eagle handed to him and began to read aloud.

'*Wednesday January the 12th. We had curly fries at lunch. Acacia threw the netball at me in PE when I wasn't looking and it bounced off my face and everyone laughed. Now my face hurts. I hate everything.*'

'Oh!' said Miss Eagle.

'Oh my days,' said Acacia.

'*Bof!*' said Ariadne Ocean Dupree.

Nishat squeaked, knocking over her chair as she jumped to her feet. 'My diary!' she wailed.

Then she covered her face and ran sobbing from the room.

It was awful. Even worse than being a 0/10, which still niggled at the back of my head behind my left ear, like a scratch or a scar. Miss Eagle made us sit in silence till someone owned up to stealing Nishat's diary and putting it in her copy of *A Midsummer Night's Dream* for Halid to read. Except no one did, and then we all had to go to Geography.

'I'm very disappointed, Seven E,' Miss Eagle said as we put our chairs away in gloomy silence. 'I thought much better of you. All of you. Bullying behaviour . . . unkindness . . . I won't have it in my classroom. Perhaps we won't be able to do this play after all.'

'At least we won't have to do the scary auditions,' whispered Efe, looking deeply relieved as we climbed the stairs.

'Hm,' said Georgie.

77

Nishat sniffled all the way through Mr Cole telling us about oxbow lakes.

Luckily, at the end of the day, something came along I could definitely fix. After school Georgie went off to her Dance Magic class thing and Billie had garden club, so it was just me and the twin Sams walking home.

They rode their bikes extra slow and in circles so I could keep up.

'I've brought KitKats,' said Sam. 'For your spell. I hid them so the lunch-box thief wouldn't gobble them all up. Two ordinary and one Chunky – because everyone knows Chunky is best.'

Everyone did.

'So what do you want me to do?'

Sam looked at her brother and her face went a bit red.

'Um. Well. You know periods? I haven't had any yet. But Efe has, and it looks super-annoying. Like, you have to remember to carry stuff with you in case it happens by surprise, and it might get on your clothes, and also it means you go hairy and get massive boobies, maybe.'

'Oh,' I said, because I was more expecting her to ask for a magic potion to make someone turn green overnight, or to make her dog talk. Also it seemed a funny conversation to have with a person you hardly knew and her twin brother.

But the boy Sam didn't seem bothered. He just nodded sympathetically about the super-annoying part.

'So I was thinking I could *not* have them. At least, for a bit. I want to try out for the Kensal Rise Kestrels – that's the under-fourteens football team – and I think having massive boobies wouldn't help.'

It seemed like it counted as good magic, because it was personal and it would make her happy, so I said yes and took the KitKats, and promised to do the spell that night, just in case there were periods lurking, ready to pop out before I had the chance.

My book didn't have any of the right sort of spells in, but I looked on the internet and the *History of Witches* place said that, in olden times, people thought pineapples would stop you having

a wee, so I decided to start there and make my
own recipe.

POTION FOR SAM
Pineapple
Watermelon
Tomato ketchup
Worcester sauce
Three blades of grass

'Why grass?' asked Georgie, peering at my list
when she got home.

'Because she's a footballer, and that adds extra
motivation,' I explained.

We didn't have any watermelon, so I put in a
whole tin of pineapple and gave the ketchup bottle
an extra-hard squeeze. Then we whizzed it all up
in Mina's fancy juice blender.

It came out lumpy and looking a bit like sick.
It smelled awful too: very sweet but slightly
gone off.

'Are you sure you want to give her that?' asked
Georgie nervously as I poured it into two empty
jam jars.

'Not yet. It still needs a secret bit of magic that only I can do or it won't work.'

Georgie narrowed her eyes. Then she sighed and went off to do her violin practice.

She's brilliant, Georgie – she's my best friend for ever and my best new sister and I love her – but she just doesn't understand witchiness. It's sad for her, really.

I picked up the jam jars and did hard thinking about squeezing your insides very tightly. Then I did some secret whispering that only I know about, and walked in three circles, and then it was done. I screwed on the lids and put the jars in the back of the fridge, ready to take one to Sam the next day.

There was still quite a bit of the potion left.

I sniffed it.

I remembered what Sam had said about massive boobies. I tugged my collar out and peered down at the amount of boobies I've already got.

Then I did the squeezing and the whispering and the walking in circles again, and drank it all down.

It was disgusting, so I knew it was definitely going to work.

GEORGIE

On Saturday morning Jem's mum, Bridget, collected Jem, Tilly and Noah, and took them off for their visitation weekend.

I didn't mind. I had my own plans for the day: violin practice, piano, stretches, and practising the new jazz routine Miss Adjoa had given us at Dance Magic. But first I was going to read all of *A Midsummer Night's Dream*. That way I'd know it really well and wouldn't be nervous about being in it, maybe.

But when I lay down on my bed and opened the big Hogwarty book of plays, there was a gentle tapping sound on my door. It was Joel.

'Hey. How are you doing, kiddo? Do you have plans for the day?'

'Yes,' I said, pointing at the book and hoping he would go away.

He came all the way in then, and perched awkwardly on the edge of my desk.

I felt a bit shy, even though I was in my own bedroom. He smelled of pine-needle man deodorant. I tried it on once, the first night we were here, just to see. I don't think it made me smell like man. Just like pine needles.

'I was wondering if you might be feeling a bit left out, maybe,' Joel said slowly.

I felt all wiggly inside. As if I'd been being talked *about*, instead of being talked *to*.

'I don't.' I held onto the book very tightly. 'Really I don't. I stopped having visitation with my dad a long time ago, and I don't miss it, or him, and I'm not jealous or left out at all.'

My face was hot. We don't talk about my dad. Not ever. It's one of our rules. We keep him a secret, as if he'd never happened to us at all.

Joel nodded. 'I'm not trying to take his place, you know,' he said. 'You've an old man already, good or bad. But . . . well. You and me, we're still getting used to this, right? All of us living together, being a family.' He looked down at his hands. 'And I reckon you're the one doing it toughest, out of all of us. Jem and the little ones, they're used to moving about, changing things.

And your ma, she chose me. She chose all this. But not you.'

'I like it, though,' I said quickly, sitting up but leaving a finger tucked into my place in the book. 'I would've chosen it.'

It wasn't completely true. Spooky had walked over my Geography homework and left muddy paw prints all over Kazakhstan. Tilly kept borrowing my hairbrush and bringing it back with the handle all bent from the effort. Noah kept borrowing my leotards for dressing up the Morrises. Even Jem had a habit of leaving her old peeled-off socks in unexpected places, like in my bed. They weren't my favourite things. But obviously I liked it.

Joel smiled. 'Well, I'm glad. But your ma thinks that you and me, we have to make a bit of an extra effort, you know? Since we don't know one another so well. And I'm not at work till six tonight, so I thought, maybe, you and me could hang out today . . . catch a movie, go bowling . . .?'

Then the doorbell rang, and Mum called up the stairs. 'Georgie, darling? There are two girls here. They say they know you from school . . .'

I put my bookmark in and hurried downstairs – to find Billie and Sam on my doorstep. Sam had a bouncy little grey dog on a lead. They both wore jeans and big puffy coats, and Billie had earmuffs in the shape of snowmen.

'Jem's not here,' I said quickly.

'Well, you are. Can you come out?' said Billie. 'We're walking the dog. And then going back to mine.'

'At the café you get free cinnamon buns,' said Sam, her eyes lighting up. 'And the pleasure of our company,' she added quickly, seeing Billie's mouth squinch up into a rose.

'Well now, who could turn that down, eh?' said Joel, appearing behind my shoulder and giving it a little squeeze.

'But . . . plans,' I mumbled, looking up at him. I meant his extra-effort plans. And mine, a little bit. And mainly that I didn't know Billie or Sam all that well, especially without Jem around to do all the hard talking parts of making friends.

But Joel found my coat and pressed my polar-bear hat into my hand and gave me a little push. 'Off you go, girls,' he said. 'You have fun now.'

And the door closed behind me without anyone asking what time I'd be back and where they lived and if their mums even knew they were here.

We walked all the way to the other end of Sorrel Street, over the bridge and into The Splendide. It had a little bell that jingled above the door, and the smells of frying bacon and hot chocolate mixed together.

'This is Georgie. She's our new friend from school,' said Billie. 'That's my brother Raffy.'

There was a boy behind the counter: a grown-up teenager boy, about seventeen, with lots of big twists of hair and a wide, soft smile.

'Uh-oh, Georgie,' he said, leaning over the counter and giving me a serious look. 'Did this one promise you free cakes, free drinks? Because you have to earn it, you know ... scrub the floor ... wash the plates ... Here's your apron ...'

'Oh! Um. OK,' I said, feeling my face go scarlet as he held one out.

'Raff-*y*,' said Billie.

He kept it up for a moment longer – then grinned as he snatched it away. 'Go on, sit – I'll bring the usual.'

My face was still glowing as we sat at a little table tucked away at the back. We had two swirly pastries with white icing dripped on the top ('They're yesterday's, but they're fine really,' Billie explained) and a can of Coke between us.

Then we went through a peely-painted blue door next to the café, and upstairs to Billie's flat. She had a bedroom right at the top, with a sloped ceiling just like mine, except hers had lots of Disney posters on the walls and very old wallpaper underneath. It was neat and tidy like mine too.

Billie flopped onto her bed. Sam flopped next to her and scooped the dog into her lap. He was called Surprise, and was quite licky if you had just eaten some swirly pastries.

'You can sit down – you don't have to ask,' said Billie; not unkindly, but with a curious look, as if I was being very strange.

I probably am very strange in other people's houses where I'm not quite sure of the rules.

'So,' said Sam, looking me up and down critically. 'Tell us about Jem.'

'Is she *really* a witch?' said Billie.

'Or is she just kind of . . . showy-offy?' said Sam.

'She's not showy-offy!' I said. 'Jem doesn't care what other people think. She's not unusual on purpose, to get attention. She just *is*.'

Billie tilted her head thoughtfully. 'Raffy's a bit like that. My other brothers, they're quiet and they think a lot. But Raffy just has things happen around him all the time. He doesn't try to make them happen, but they *do*.'

At that exact moment there was an urgent steady beeping sound from below, muffled through all the floors, accompanied by a strong smell of smoke.

'Should we—?' I said.

But a minute later there was a thudding up the stairs and a cheerful shout from below: 'No drama! Just a bit of a tiny being-on-fire situation in the kitchen, innit. Sorted now.'

'See?' said Billie.

'I do,' I said, thinking of Mediterranean herbs and vases. 'I really do.'

'Do *you* think she's a witch?' asked Sam, narrowing her eyes.

'Erm,' I said. '*She* definitely thinks she's a witch. And she says that's all you need really. Like, if you believe in it enough, it's true.'

'Hmph,' said Billie, flopping back down on the bed. 'Enough about her. Tell us about *you*.'

I felt my face going scarlet again. 'I'm not so interesting,' I mumbled. I fiddled with my boring plaits and my boring shoes and my boring neat white socks.

'Pffrt,' said Sam. 'Everyone's interesting.'

'Especially people who are mysterious,' said Billie, her eyes wide and warm. 'Like, we know all about your sister. But we don't know anything about you.'

'You've got Hidden Depths,' said Sam.

'Sorry,' I said.

But they didn't mean it in a bad way. They seemed to like it.

So I told them about Dance Magic, and violin Grade Five, and they didn't think that was boring. So then I told them about suddenly living with a new dad-shaped person who wanted to be your friend when you were trying to read your book, and how Mum invented Fairy Dusters and sometimes it's as if she likes Fairy Dusters more than she likes me, and how it was a bit hard to suddenly be a sister, actually, when it meant muddy footprints on Kazakhstan and rabbits in leotards. Once I started talking I couldn't seem to stop.

'See?' said Sam, grinning. 'Hidden Depths.'

And then we went and played on Billie's brothers' PlayStation, even though we weren't allowed, and I loved it, I loved it, I loved it.

JEM

Dear Georgie,

Don't be lonely without us today. We will have a rubbish time with Mum, I promise. She will lock us in her flat and make us polish things because everything in Croydon is shiny. And we definitely won't go out for burgers or anything.

Also remember to feed Spooky and change his water and kiss him on the nose, because I'm not sure your mum knows about all that yet (especially the kissing-on-the-nose).

Love from your sister Jemima Magee, aged 11¼

It felt funny leaving our new house behind, with only Dad and Mina and Georgie and Spooky in it. Like the whole last couple of weeks might not be real, and when we came back there wouldn't be any new house with the ostrich egg and my own bedroom all to myself and Georgie being my sister. I did a very quick witchy walk around, whispering kind words, just in case.

'I'm not doing anything!' said Tilly loudly when I went into her room. She had her bottom in the air and her arms buried in her shoebox doll's house, which was definitely something.

'I'm not doing anything!' said Noah, bundling all the Morrises onto a weird nest of towels and blankets and sitting on it furtively.

'Good,' I said, unconvinced. Then I packed the overnight bag that has everyone's pants in, because sometimes, if you leave it to Dad, he forgets, and then Mum phones him up to shout at him.

At ten o'clock Mum's car zoomed up outside, and we all piled in.

Our mum, Bridget, has bright blue eyes and blonde hair (short like mine but curlier), and a big loud laugh like a bell. She always wears swoopy black eyeliner and purple lipstick, and lots of silver earrings all the way up her ears, like she isn't old at all. Today she was wearing a gothy purple dress with silver spider's webs on it, stripy tights and huge boots. She had her favourite patchouli perfume on too. My mum is where I get all my witchiness from. It's our special bond that only we have – even more than her just being my mum.

I've never seen her do a spell exactly. But she has special crystals with names like Serenity and Happiness that she puts in her handbag to give her good fortune. She tucked Courage into my skirt pocket on my first day at school. She's got a book called *Big Magic* on the shelf by her bed. Anyway, you don't have a bat tattoo and a black cat called Spooky without something being up.

'Well now,' she said, looking up at the house with a grin. 'Fallen on your feet there, Joel.'

'Georgie did our hair,' said Noah, who was wearing his in two tight French plaits again. Tilly's was in a ginormous round bun with frizzy edges.

'And don't you look fancy!'

Mum ruffled my hair, which usually I don't like but today I didn't mind, and flashed me a smile. Then we drove away with Paramore playing extra-loud on the CD player and all of us singing along.

We went to Lloyd Park, and Noah headed into the adventure playground while Tilly followed him around, glaring at anyone who tried to push in on the queue for the slides.

We played frisbee golf and Mum won.

We had milkshakes and dipped chips in them.

Then Mum parked in the multi-storey and we went to the shoppingy bit of Croydon, which is a big loud mall with boring clothes and no fun shops at all except one toy shop and one charity shop, and we didn't have any money anyway.

But Tilly didn't seem to mind. She mooched round and round a shop full of little necklaces and purses, and frilly knickers with flamingos on. Eventually she settled on a brooch: a huge gold one shaped like a butterfly, all sparkly, with little blue and yellow crystals set into the wings.

'Oh!' said Mum when she saw it. 'We'll all see you coming, eh, love?'

Tilly shook her hair. 'It's not for *me*. It's for my *beloved*. I'm glad I've fallen in love with a girl one this time,' she said. 'Boy presents are never sparkly.'

'I know,' sighed Noah, his eyes big as he looked at the racks of twinkly rings.

'There's no such thing as boy presents,' said me and Mum, both at the same time, and giggled.

That happens a lot. Dad says it's because we're much too alike, but I think it's because we're connected on the astral plane.

Then her mobile phone rang. 'Oh!' she said again, her eyes bright as she read the screen. 'I'll just be outside, love.' She hurried off to answer it.

I took the ugly brooch. 'It's twelve pounds, Tills,' I said gently.

'I know,' said Tilly, pushing past everyone to the counter. She reached into her coat pockets and produced handful after handful of coins: five ps, two ps, a few fifty ps, all in a big heaping pile on the counter.

The sleepy-eyed man behind the counter looked like he might cry.

'It's all there,' said Tilly. 'Twelve pounds exactly. I counted it. Twice.'

The sleepy-eyed man sighed and began to count it out himself, very slowly, while the people queuing behind us all made shuffly tutting noises.

'Where did you get twelve pounds?' I hissed, pulling Tilly's hood – we didn't get very much pocket money and Tilly had always spent hers before she'd even got it.

'You know I said I was doing a sponsored silence at school so I wouldn't have to talk to people? Well, they all gave me money. Loads of money. And I couldn't tell them not to because I was busy being silent.'

'Tilly! That's meant for charity, then! You can't just spend it on *you*!'

'I'm not spending it on me. I'm spending it on the postie. It's a present. That's sort of like charity.'

I looked for Mum because I knew she wouldn't think so, either. But she was still outside the shop, on the phone, laughing, her face all lit up and happy.

I knew who she'd be talking to. A new man-friend.

My heart went all twisty.

It's not like I don't want her to be happy, but it would be nice if it was because of *us*.

'Please,' said Tilly, tugging my sleeve. 'Please let me buy it.'

'Please,' said Noah as well, rubbing his face on my arm.

And I decided they'd probably had enough disappointing things happen to them, so if Tilly wanted to buy an ugly sparkly butterfly because she was in love, then that was fine by me.

That night, after the littles had gone to bed, Mum made us cocoa with cinnamon and a pinch of cloves. It's her special recipe. A potion, really. (She says it isn't, but she stirs the cups three times widdershins, just like me, so I know better.)

We sat in her little kitchen, just us big ones.

'So. The new place. Is it really so terrible, honeybun?' asked Mum, licking her spoon.

'Agony,' I said. 'Dad makes us eat couscous, even though everyone knows it's just big sand. There's hardly any carpets – it's all bare floor-boards with rugs on so we'll probably get splinters. There's a huge hairy man from Fairy Dusters called Janusz who comes round and does cleaning once a week, and he hoovered up Doris Morris and she had to be rescued out of the bag, all covered in fluff. And Mina was totally unimpressed with the half a mouse Spooky left on her pillow, when every-one knows he does it out of love. It was the bottom half, though. It's nicer when they've still got a face.'

Only I don't think Mum was listening properly because she said it all sounded very *nice*, and that we were *lucky*, and how she was pleased we were *happy* – as if I hadn't said it was bad at all.

'You're happy as well, though,' I said. 'I can tell. Your hair's gone shiny and you keep doing little smiles about nothing.'

She did one just then. 'Don't be daft.' Then she blushed and patted her hair.

It did look bouncy. Her whole face looked softer. She's always been quite a round person, like me, but she seemed a tiny bit rounder now, as if someone had been taking her out for lots of posh dinners.

'You can tell us if there's a new man-friend,' I said, sipping my cocoa. 'We won't be cross. Or – if anyone is cross, I'll make them not be.'

'Jemima – honey – you can't *make* people not be cross,' she said, which just goes to show that not everyone realizes quite how clever I am at witchiness – even my mum, who should know best of everyone. 'But I don't have a new fella around, I swear to you.'

Then she looked at the clock and gulped down the rest of her cocoa in three big glugs. 'Sleepy!' she said, doing a big yawn. 'Early start in the morning!'

The next day she was up at seven, and she shooed us off the sofa bed where all three of us slept before Noah was even awake. She was wearing tight purple leggings with silver stars, trainers instead of her usual clumpy boots, and there was a big heavy bag zipped up and waiting by the door, as if she'd packed to go on holiday.

'I've got a little something of my own to do this morning, so I'll pop you back to your dad's now,' she said. 'You don't need breakfast, do you?'

We did, because we *always* did: boiled eggs and toasty soldiers, which was her best cooking.

Tilly glared out from under her hair.

Noah looked up at me sleepily, his hair still in its two plaits, now surrounded by a halo of fuzz.

But Mum was jingling her car keys in her hand, hopping from foot to foot.

'It's fine,' I said quietly, because I would *make* it fine.

We all got in the car, still in our pyjamas.

'I won't come in,' she said, zooming up to the front of the new house and checking her watch. Then she zoomed off without looking back.

'Do you think Mina will make us boiled eggs and toasty soldiers?' said Noah in a small voice.

'We can make them ourselves,' I promised.

I opened the door with my own personal door key, which I have because I'm the oldest Magee (which still matters, even if Georgie is, like, a tiny bit older).

The house was very quiet.

All the curtains were still pulled shut.

I went up to ask if Georgie wanted breakfast too – but her bed was empty. It didn't seem to have been slept in at all.

I ran to my room, thinking she'd probably missed me so much she'd decided to sleep there – but it was empty and unslept in too. She wasn't in Tilly's or Noah's either.

'Kidnap! Murder! *FIRE!*' I yelled, because at least one of those had to have happened, and also they are good words for waking people up.

'Where?' yelled Tilly, peering up the stairs.

'Nooo!' wailed Noah, sprinting for his room to rescue all the Morrises.

'Whuh?' said Dad, stumbling out of their bedroom in his pants, with his hair all sticking up.

'It's Georgie!' I shouted. 'She's missing!' – just as the front door swung open with a bang.

'No, I'm not,' said Georgie, looking up at me from the doorstep. 'I'm right here.'

'Hooray, you aren't kidnapped! Or on fire!'

Then there was a loud beeping noise from the kitchen, and it turned out the toast was, a bit.

We put a damp tea towel over the toaster, and the flames went out right away. Then Mina came down in her silky dressing gown, with no make-up on and looking sort of yoghurty.

'Lovely Sunday lie-in – just what I wanted,' she muttered.

I wrapped Georgie in a hug, just in case she disappeared again.

'I can't believe you thought I got kidnapped!' she said. 'I went over to Billie's, to see her café and eat pastries. Then Sam invited me for a sleepover. It was brilliant, Jemmy! We stayed up till half past three, and then her mum told us she was going to dangle us out of the window by our ankles if she didn't shut the bleep up. One of her mums. She's got two. Not like we do, though. They kissed and everything.'

'Oh. Did Sam feel sorry for you?' I said – quietly so she wouldn't get upset. 'Because you were by yourself?'

Georgie shook her head, and a little crinkle appeared between her eyebrows. 'No. Sam says I've got Hidden Depths. We talked about school. And Miss Eagle. And the play! And then she had football practice, so I had to come home early.'

'Oh,' I said. 'Well. That's really . . . nice.'

It *was* nice. Georgie *does* have Hidden Depths. It's just that mostly *I* am the person who notices that.

There wasn't time for me to say so, though, because just at that moment there was a huge scream, even louder than when I was shouting *FIRE!* to wake everyone up.

We all ran into the back room to see.

'Look!' cried Mina, wrapping her dressing gown tightly around herself and pointing a perfectly shiny red fingernail at the mantelpiece.

We all looked.

There was the vase, the clock, a photograph of Georgie as a baby, another vase, Dad's giraffe . . .

Then an empty space.

'The ostrich egg!' said Mina in a high cracked voice. 'It's gone!'

GEORGIE

We all stood round the mantelpiece, staring at the empty space where the ostrich egg wasn't.

'It wasn't me!' said Noah.

'It wasn't any of us!' said Tilly.

'We weren't here,' said Jem.

'None of us were,' I said, frowning.

We all looked at Joel, who was wearing a very small pair of pants with Daffy Duck on them, so I tried very hard to look at his face instead.

'Well, don't all look at me,' he said. 'It's an egg. Why would I take an egg?'

'Well, *someone* has,' whispered Mum.

She was quivering. I knew why. Mum would be in awful trouble if it really *was* lost. Every time we went to Granny's, one of the aunts would ask if we were looking after the precious family heirlooms – which meant, *We're still cross that Grandpa gave them to you, not us.* They all thought that Mum should have moved back in with Granny after what happened with Dad. And they definitely didn't think she should live with a divorced man with a crinkly face and three children. I used to think that once you were an adult, no one told you off any more, but it isn't true. You just get to go back to your own house afterwards and open a bottle of wine to make you feel better.

Mum looked at Jem and Tilly and Noah very sternly. 'It's very important to me, that egg,' she said in a quiet voice. 'And if it was damaged because someone was playing a silly game . . . or knocked it over because they were messing about . . . I would like to know. Now.'

I hoped and hoped that it wasn't them.

'But we weren't here!' said Jem, stamping her foot and moving slightly in front of the little two like a shield.

'I mean, they really weren't, Mina, love . . .' said Joel, wrapping his arms round his nude middle and looking very cold.

'Then perhaps it went missing before this weekend! And we just didn't notice, hmm?'

Everyone looked at everyone else.

'Burglars?' suggested Tilly.

'Think they'd have picked up a few other bits and bobs while they were at it,' said Joel gently. 'It's not that valuable.'

'It's priceless!' wailed Mum, and burst into tears.

Joel caught my eye, then took her away for a cup of tea and some unburnt breakfast.

We all stayed in the back room, staring at the egg gap.

'How much money is *priceless*?' whispered Noah, clutching Boris Morris very tightly.

'A lot more than all our pocket money, added up, for years and years,' said Jem.

'Oh,' said Noah, his eyes going wide.

Spooky wandered in, his tail waving, and leaped easily from the floor to the sofa to the mantelpiece, his tail brushing the glittery twigs in the vase and sending a sparkly shower onto the floor. He paused for a moment, blinking crossly. Then he sneezed.

'Oh!' I gasped. 'Spooky – he couldn't have . . .?'

Jem glared at me and scooped him up, clutching him tightly as his limbs splayed out like a furry starfish.

'As if he would,' she said crossly. 'He knows he's not allowed to climb on everything. And even if he did,' she added – as he wriggled and escaped back onto the nearest bookshelf, setting another vase rocking – 'he'd have left a mess, wouldn't he? There'd be egg everywhere.'

That was a good point.

'Oh!' said Jem. 'Maybe the ghosts came back.'

'It's not ghosts,' I said, because it wasn't.

'It could be ghosts. Or fairies.'

'Or . . . the hairy cleaner . . .' said Tilly slowly.

'Janusz!' said Jem. 'From Fairy Dusters. Ohhhh.'

Janusz the cleaner came on Thursdays. We all thought very hard, trying to remember if we'd seen the egg since he was here with his duster and squirty vinegar smells – but no one could be completely sure.

'Next time he comes we'll follow him around,' said Jem. 'He's bound to give himself away.'

'Hmm,' said Noah.

Then he went upstairs, and wouldn't come out of his bedroom for the whole of the rest of the day.

'Post-visitation woe,' said Tilly knowledgeably as she slid cream crackers under his bedroom door, one by one, followed by a knife with a smear of butter, and another holding a slice of cheese. 'We all get it.'

She sighed heavily, then went off to write a poem called *The Unbearable Bleakness of Childhood*.

'Does Noah miss his mum horribly?' I asked, perching on Jem's window seat.

'Not really,' said Jem. 'He was very small when she left. He's more used to her being gone than being at home.'

'Do *you* miss her horribly?'

Jem came to sit next to me, resting her head on my shoulder. 'Only when she's being rubbish at mumming, and having secret man-friends,' she said, sighing. 'It's always the same. They start out being all nice and sexy-faced, and good at remembering to buy flowers or whatever it is mums like about boyfriends. Then, after a couple of weeks of her being all distracted, they decide she's too weird, or too loud, or too lumpy round the middle, or they remember that actually they have a wife and probably you don't need a girlfriend as well. Then she spends all weekend in bed crying eyeliner all over her pillows. She always buys good biscuits then, though – chocolate ones with foil on. So it could be worse.' She wriggled round so her back was to me, and handed me her hairbrush. 'When do you think you'll want to kiss someone?'

'Not for ages,' I said, brushing out a chunk of her hair so I could add a tiny plait. 'I'm going to wait until I fall in love, hopefully. And I don't want to do that until I've passed Grade Eight violin, because it's distracting. Everyone says. You?'

Jem hummed. 'Don't know. It would be handy to get it out of the way, I reckon. But not soon.'

'Are you going to kiss boys or girls? I think boys.'

'I think both,' said Jem, yelping softly as I tugged out a knot. 'Like, I like sewing, and I like knitting, and I like drawing. I wouldn't want to have to pick just one.'

We both agreed to not marry anyone at all until we were thirty-three, and only if the other one thought we'd found someone absolutely nice and sexy-faced.

By Monday I was looking forward to school again, now that I had Sam and Billie as proper friends of my own, not just Jem's who let me tag along. So long as no one was going to mark me out of ten, or steal my diary, or my crisps.

In English, Miss Eagle had draped different-coloured cloths over all the windows, so there was a soft pinkish and bluish light glowing through them. She'd spread rugs and cushions in a circle on the floor. There was soft music playing, and a smelly candle burning on her desk. It felt like being in a really big tent, only with desks in it and a gap for where the fire extinguisher was.

'Are we doing the play, miss?' asked Big Mohammad.

'I'm not sitting on the floor, miss,' said Madison. 'There's germs.'

'I'm not being in that play, miss,' said Alfie. 'There's fairies in that play.'

'For real?' asked Halid.

'I googled it,' said Alfie.

Halid shook his head sadly. 'I can't be in no fairy play, miss.'

Miss Eagle took a long deep breath through her nose, looking down at her buckle shoes. Then she looked up again with a bright firm smile on her red-lipsticky mouth.

'Actually, Seven E, we're not going to talk about the play today – though I'm very excited to hear you were interested enough to do some research, Alfie, and we'll talk a little bit more about fairies another time. Today, as you can probably guess, we're going to do something rather different from a usual English class. Sit. Relax. I promise there aren't any germs, Madison – or none that will hurt you.'

I found a cushion and sat down next to Jem.

Miss Eagle knelt down in the circle too. 'Now, we all know that some strange, unkind, upsetting things have been happening at school,' she said, smoothing her skirt.

'*Cute, but a bit up himself,*' murmured Alfie.

Nishat sniffled.

'*Zut alors,*' murmured Ariadne Ocean Dupree.

'But it made me think about how you all might be feeling, and how important it is for you to feel safe and comfortable when you're in my classroom. We're going to be working on drama together this term, and that means we need trust.'

'I ain't falling into no one's arms, miss,' said Acacia, who was sitting in a chair at the back of the circle.

'You won't have to,' said Miss Eagle with a smile. 'Not today, anyway! I thought we should start by sharing how we feel right now. I'll start. I feel . . . disappointed.'

'Worried,' said Efe.

'Stressed,' said Sam.

'Suspicious,' said Billie.

'Scared,' said lots of people, all together.

'Curious,' said Jem.

I didn't say anything.

'Thank you, everyone. That's a really brave and important thing to do – though it's fine if you chose not to, as well,' she added quickly so that I wouldn't feel awful. 'It can really help to express yourself. I feel quite free. As if I've let something go, and don't have to think about it any more.'

Miss Eagle clasped her hands together on her lap.

'We all have secrets. Every single one of us. Things we're ashamed of. Things we've done. Words we've said, or wished we'd said. Fears.

Problems, and worries. Hopes too; our ambitions or dreams or deep desires.'

There was a little ripple of smirky laughing around the circle.

Miss Eagle nodded. 'Yes, that's exactly what I'm talking about. You're laughing because you're embarrassed. *Oh gosh, not me, I don't have any deep desires! I don't have worries!* But we all do. And we're all afraid of being found out. And that's no way to live, is it?'

It was as if she was talking just to me.

Just to me, and Mum.

But everyone went quiet.

'Nah, miss,' said Big Mohammad softly.

'Nah indeed. So we're going to do the same thing with our secrets. Well, not quite the same; we won't share them. Not out loud. But I'm going to leave this special post box on my desk all this week and next so that anyone can share a secret they want to be free of.'

She fetched a shiny green ball from her desk, with a slit cut in it like a post box. It was papier-mâché – the sort you make by wrapping bits of paper round a balloon and popping it when it's dry. Then she handed out small slips of yellow paper, blank, about the size of the joke you get in a cracker. Everyone got one.

'As you can see, no one can take the secrets out. No one can see in. The box will stay in my classroom, behind my desk, and you can come at any time of the school day to post your secret. And next week, on Friday, we'll have a special ceremony to send those anxious secret feelings up in smoke!'

JEM

Dear Billie and Sam,

Thank you for being kind and looking after Georgie while I was busy with my mum.

You could totally invite me over to your house any time, if you like. I am good at sleepovers. I would do any magic spells you wanted, and you wouldn't have to give me any KitKats at all. And I would be excellent at being in a play, probably, if I wanted to be.

From your friend Jemima Magee, aged 11¼

'Can *I* put a secret in the special green post box?' asked Noah at breakfast the next morning.

'Nope. You haven't got a slip of yellow paper,' I told him, shaking Cheerios out into my bowl.

'I would put in that I want to marry the postie, even if she didn't like the butterfly brooch I gave her and thinks I'm weird,' said Tilly.

'It's not a secret if everyone knows it, love,' said Dad, passing me the milk.

'I'm not sure about this teacher of yours,' said Mina, pursing her mouth as she bit into her sawdusty breakfast crackers. 'Gosh, this jam is unusual. Rather tart.'

My eyes popped wide open.

There, in the middle of the table, was a jar filled with lumpy pineapple mush and a few barely visible flecks of green. The second jar of Sam's magic potion that I'd left in the fridge. Now spread all over Mina's breakfast.

'Anyway,' she went on, 'if there are problems with bullying and stealing and breaking the rules, they should be dealt with appropriately. Suspensions; detentions. Not this arty-farty, touchy-feely stuff.'

Georgie fiddled with her spoon. 'It's OK, Mum. I'm not putting a secret in.'

Mina set her coffee mug down with a bit too much of a thump.

I knew why. Georgie's secret is massive. Obviously she's told me, because of us being best friends, but she's never supposed to tell anyone ever. Even Tilly and Noah don't know about it.

'Hey – did I tell you who I caught on the late shift?' said Dad, reaching across the table to squeeze Mina's hand. 'A criminal syndicate of Pringles rustlers. They tuck the tubes up their sleeves and down their trousers, and go hobbling out of the shop like the Tin Man. Rounded up six of them just this morning. Especially fond of barbecue flavour, they are.'

And we spent the rest of breakfast arguing about which flavour was best, even though everyone knows it's the red ones.

'It'll be fine,' I told Georgie confidently, clearing away the breakfast things. 'The magic won't make her ill or anything. Your mum already has periods. I think. She's definitely got boobies. It'll just be like she's eaten some weird jam with grass in. Not magic.'

But I took the jar upstairs and hid it in my jumper drawer. Just in case.

*

At lunch everyone wanted to talk about Miss Eagle's secrets ball.

'Do you think she'll read them? Even though she said she wouldn't?' asked Efe.

'She wouldn't,' said Billie.

'*I* would,' said Sam.

'I would try really hard not to,' said Billie, 'but then I would have, like, a little peep. And then I would wish I hadn't. Secrets are stupid; no one should have them.' She looked in her lunch box and sighed. 'I had a whole almond croissant in here this morning.'

'I don't have any,' I said.

'Almond croissants?' asked Efe.

'Secrets,' I said. I really don't. I don't like hiding things.

They all looked amazed, except for Georgie; maybe even a little bit jealous. I liked that.

'I'm putting one in the post-box thing, anyway,' said Sam, chomping on an apple. 'Because she's going to set it on fire, and I like fires.'

'She won't know whose secret is whose, even if she does read them,' said Billie slowly.

'Teachers know everyone's handwriting,' Georgie said, looking anxious. 'Always.'

Sam sniffed. 'I'll do block capitals. Or write with my left hand.'

'We all should,' said Billie. 'All of us together.'

'Promise?' said Sam. She put out her hand.

Billie and Efe put their hands in over the picnic table too, like they were making a pact.

Georgie's eyes fluttered anxiously to mine. Then she took a deep breath, and very slowly reached her hand out as well.

I couldn't believe it.

I never care what anyone else thinks. But suddenly I really, really wanted to put my hand in too.

'You could make something up,' Georgie said helpfully.

'That's cheating,' said Efe quietly.

So they all put their hands in together without me, and Sam said, 'Three, two, one—' and they threw their hands up in the air while I ate my sandwich.

I definitely didn't really mind. I completely forgot all about it immediately.

Especially on Thursday, when I left Georgie behind for orchestra practice and raced home from school to be a spy.

Janusz the hairy Fairy Duster was already there, with his pinny and rubber gloves on, dusting all the millions of vases, while Tilly and Noah followed him around.

'We've left a trap for him,' whispered Tilly through her hair. 'To see if he steals it, like he stole the ostrich egg.'

'Treasure,' said Noah.

'Irresistible treasure,' added Tilly.

The treasure turned out to be Horace Morris the brontosaurus, perched on the end of Noah's bed wearing Mina's favourite necklace: a silver string with delicate purple droplets hanging off it.

'You can't try to get him to steal that!' I hissed, dragging them both back onto the landing as Janusz thumped the vacuum cleaner savagely up the stairs. 'Mina would be so upset!'

Also she would never be able to give it to me as a gift for a new sort-of daughter who she'd decided she definitely liked.

But Janusz didn't steal the necklace. He just grunted, set Horace Morris carefully on Noah's bedside table, and vacuum-cleanered everything in sight, including the wallpaper and the curtains. An hour later he left – without stealing anything at all.

'He probably knew we were watching,' said Tilly. 'We'll get him next week. Catch him red-handed.'

'Unless it wasn't him who took the egg,' I said.

'Hmm,' said Noah, and he went and climbed into his newly made, perfectly neat bed with the covers pulled up over his ears.

I took the necklace off Horace Morris and slipped into the cool, quiet, white space of Mina and Dad's bedroom. (I put it around my neck first, for safekeeping.)

Their bedroom has white walls, and floaty white curtains, and silky white bed things with a white furry rug on top, and a beigey carpet. It was like being in a hotel; a really spendy one with those little soaps in wrappers.

But today there was a little pile of things on the bed. Bras. Three bras in different colours: a lacy black one, a padded one in bright blue satin, and a white one with roses on.

'Oh!' said Mina as she came in and found me.

I squeaked and dropped the lacy black bra – which I had just sort of picked up out of curiosity while I was passing and held against my front.

'I'm not doing anything! I just . . . I was just going past and . . .'

I fingered the necklace hidden under my school shirt, but I didn't really know how to tell her it was there without having to explain about Janusz, and then she'd remember about the egg and be all upset again.

But Mina tilted her head kindly. 'I understand, sweetheart. They *are* pretty. I wonder . . .' She held the blue one up against me. 'Maybe not. The colour's perfect for you, though. Perhaps we should go shopping one day, hmm? Get you a few special new things, have some girly chats . . . if Bridget wouldn't mind . . .'

'She wouldn't,' I said quickly.

Mina smiled. 'I'll have a look at my diary, see when I can slot you in. And, oh dear, off to the charity bag with these – they just don't fit me any more!' She scooped up the bras and carried them away.

I had to go and have a bit of a lie-down after that. Obviously I already knew I was a super-powerful witch. Obviously. But what if Sam's potion had made Mina's boobies start vanishing already?

And what would happen if she found out it was me who'd done it?

She definitely wouldn't like me then. And we'd never go for girly chats at all, not ever.

I put the necklace back where it belonged. I emptied the leftover jar of potion down the toilet (it took two flushes to make it all go down). Then I changed out of my uniform, and went and knocked on Sam's door, over the road.

One of her mums opened it. She had oblong glasses and short, bright blue hair.

'Hello! I'm Jem, from the house opposite, and I very urgently need to see Sam! The girl one.'

'Shh!' said the woman, looking cross. Then she beckoned me inside, and shooed me all the way down the hall and into the kitchen. I suddenly had a worry about Stranger Danger and how I was now locked in someone's house who I'd never met – but then I saw Sam playing with the dog in the back garden, and that made it OK.

'Sorry,' said the blue-haired woman, suddenly going un-cross and smiling. 'My wife's at work in her office at the front.'

'I know,' I said. 'On the golden sofas. Talking to sad people.'

Georgie had told me all about them. One of the mums was Dr Paget, who did family therapy in their front room. This one had to be Dr Skidelsky.

She raised an eyebrow. 'Well, aren't you well-informed . . .? It just means that chit-chat in the hallway is very much not allowed. I like your skirt. Would you like a coffee?'

'I don't like coffee. And it's good, isn't it? I made it myself. The skirt, I mean.'

I swished it round my thighs to show it off. It was all strips of different fabrics cut on an angle, and it swirled outwards. There was one place where there was a hole, and another place where you could see my sewing had gone a bit wrong, and it was a bit bunchy round the waist. But I was still really proud of it. No one else had one anything like it in the whole world.

Also I was in Sam's house, just like Georgie had been.

'Sam! You've got a guest!' yelled Dr Skidelsky, opening the back door.

I hurried outside.

Sam stood in the garden with her arms folded, looking me up and down in a not-very-friendly way, which I supposed was OK because I wasn't exactly invited. But I was there on official business.

'Is it working? The magic I gave you. Is it . . .? Have you started . . .?' I made a twirly motion with my hand towards her insides.

'Oh!' said Sam. 'No periods. And no boobies at all – look.' She pulled her T-shirt tight across her chest so I could see.

I nodded seriously, ignoring the way my heart felt thumpy.

'How often are you taking it?'

'Twice a day. Spoonful on my muesli at breakfast, spoonful before bed. There's not much left, though. Can I have some more?'

I shook my head. 'It's very powerful. More would overdo it. I mean, you'll want boobies one day, right?'

'I will never, ever want boobies,' sighed Sam. 'Can you do me a spell to make me taller? Taller than my brother? For ever? I'll give you KitKats. Six KitKats.'

'I'll think about it.'

But I wasn't going to. When you are as powerful as me, you can't just go around making people taller. You should only do things that matter. Things that make everything better for everyone.

When I got back to my bedroom, I hunted through my backpack until I found it: my yellow slip of paper. I wrote down my secret. Because, to be completely totally honest and truthful, I did have one really. I think I always knew I did.

Something I hoped no one would ever find out.

Something that might spoil everything for ever.

Something so secret, even Georgie didn't know it.

Then I folded it up and put it in my left shoe, ready to take to Miss Eagle, so she could burn it and set me free for ever.

GEORGIE

Two things happened the next week.

First, Sam's mum Dr Skidelsky came to school in the middle of assembly to complain to Mrs Cooper, the head teacher, about her utter failure to respond to the 'lunch-box crime wave' that was affecting our class.

'So embarrassing,' said Sam, putting her jumper over her head.

Her brother turned even redder than even I do.

It worked for a day or two. But slowly an apple here and a sandwich there began to disappear again.

Then, on Friday, Miss Eagle held a very special English class.

For a whole half-hour we had an ordinary English lesson about verbs. We all did very badly, because no one could stop staring at the shiny green ball with the letter-box slit sitting on her desk. Miss Eagle even seemed to have dressed to match it, in a stiff green brocade dress with a sticky-out skirt, and a little red cardigan and red patent shoes.

'Miss, are you going to let us do the ball-of-secrets thing today, like you said?' asked Big Mohammad eventually.

'It is totally false advertising to make us do verbs, miss,' said Lianne.

'And you said we was building trust and, like, feeling safe in your class,' added Alfie.

Miss Eagle smiled. 'A very fine point, Alfie. And I'm so happy to know that you've all embraced the concept so thoroughly. This is full to bursting, you know!'

She picked up the ball and shook it. There was a rustle of papers inside.

I shared a secret smile with Billie and Sam. That morning, before tutor group, we had all gone together, with Efe, to drop our secrets in.

I know I promised Mum I wouldn't, but I don't want to carry it around with me all the time. I want it to disappear in a puff of smoke, and then I'll never need to worry about anyone finding out ever again.

Jem scratched her nose and looked at the floor. I knew she felt left out. I felt awful about it. But it wasn't our fault she didn't have a secret to put inside. She's special. She's luckier than us.

'Come on then, all of you,' said Miss Eagle, standing up with a smile. 'If we're going to do this properly, we need some ceremony. And somewhere outdoors, with a bucket of water to put out the fire, just in case.'

We all pulled on coats, trooped out into the cold and gathered by the steps of the sports complex.

Madison carried a metal wastepaper bin for the fire to go into.

Halid had three bottles of NutriGenix sports drink to put out the fire.

Everyone was shuffly with excitement. It was as if all the nasty things that had been happening – the lunches going missing, and the mean four-out-of-tens stuck up on the wall, and poor Nishat's diary being stolen – it could all be put right with one struck match.

'Where's Efe?' whispered Billie, frowning as we shuffled into a semicircle.

She hadn't turned up to our English lesson at all.

'Gather round, come on,' said Miss Eagle, standing at the top of the steps, the bin at her feet, the green ball in her hand. 'Sensibly, please! No pushing! Now, this collection of secrets—'

There was the sound of running feet, and Efe came sprinting round the corner, her long coat flapping behind her. 'Miss, miss – wait, miss, don't start burning things without me—'

Miss Eagle turned round.

Efe skidded to a halt – as Miss Eagle took a step backwards.

Off the steps.

Her red patent shoe seemed to hang in the air for one horrible, endless, frozen second.

Then she fell backwards, hard, onto the concrete.

She screamed. Not even just once. Again and again – short sharp screams.

I clapped my hand over my mouth.

For what seemed like a terribly long time, no one moved.

Then Big Mohammad stepped forward, and Alfie and Madison and Acacia and Billie.

'Miss, miss – it's all right, miss,' said Big Mohammad, kneeling down and holding Miss Eagle's hand, even though she was a teacher.

'We'll look after you, miss,' said Alfie.

'Oh my days, that is well broken,' said Madison, looking away with her face all screwed up.

Miss Eagle was lying on her back, her dress pulled sideways so you could see her bra and the top of her chest, and her left foot twisted round at a sickening angle.

Nishat screamed.

Halid looked like he was going to cry.

I wanted to do something helpful that wasn't screaming or crying, but all my brain would do was think, *She's broken her ankle! What if we can't do the play now?* – which wasn't helpful at all.

I looked frantically around for Jem – she's brilliant at knowing what to do – but then Miss Eagle started to sob and make a waily noise.

Billie pushed her way through, knelt down and said, 'It's OK, miss, I've called for an ambulance.' She carefully laid her coat over Miss Eagle like a blanket, and we all breathed a sigh of relief that there weren't any more teacher bras or chests on display.

Suddenly everyone wanted to help.

'We should put a pillow under her head,' said Edmond Hudson.

'And under her leg,' said Alfie. 'To, like, elevate it.'

'Nah, bruv, you don't move it,' said Big Mohammad. 'Not if it's broken.'

'Is it definitely broken?' said Nishat.

'Girl, her foot wasn't pointing that way this morning,' said Acacia.

'That is totally not helping,' said Sam.

'I'm really sorry,' said Efe in a tiny voice. 'I had to go to Mrs Cooper's office, to sign up for . . . um . . . never mind. Sorry.'

'So you should be,' said Madison, folding her arms and glaring. 'You practically pushed her over!'

Efe began to sniff, and then to cry.

'Completely, utterly not helping,' said Sam, rolling her eyes.

'Someone should go and wait by the gates so they can tell the ambulance where to come,' said Jem, suddenly appearing at my side as if she knew I needed her. 'Come on, Georgie, we can do that.'

She slipped her hand into mine and I followed her gratefully all the way to the gates, where it was cooler and calmer and no one was waily.

'Oh, Jem!' I whispered.

'It'll be all right,' she said firmly. 'She didn't hit her head; she just hurt her ankle and they can fix those. After school we should all go to Billie's café – we've had a shock and you need sugary tea after a shock – Dad taught me, that time Noah got his head stuck in the railings and we had to feed him bourbon biscuits through the bars till the firefighters came. And also distractions, so we should talk about other things. Um. Do you really like courgetti? Do you think you can do it the other way round? Imagine a whole courgette made out of pasta. You'd need something to stick it together, though, like honey. Or jam. Or Nutella. Maybe I won't make a courgette out of pasta. Did you understand that thing we did in Maths? With all the exes and whys? I think Maths should just be numbers. And triangles. With the occasional pie chart. I don't think it should be allowed to have letters in as well – that is English's job . . .'

I held her hand gratefully as she kept on talking about nothing much at all, till the flashing lights of the ambulance appeared.

When we got back, Mrs Cooper was there and had shooed everyone away, because a big circle of children all staring at you while you cry isn't nice for anyone, especially a teacher. But no one wanted to go back to class, so we all lined up at the top of the sports-complex steps and pretended to be looking the other way.

Miss Eagle was lifted onto a trolley and rolled into the back of the ambulance.

She gave us a little wave, like a broken queen, just before they slammed the doors closed. Her small pale hand made me feel even worse – especially when Efe burst into tears again.

'Hey, shush, come here,' said Big Mohammad, wrapping his big arm round her shoulders. 'No one's blaming you, right? Right?' He looked around the circle, not good-sense-of-humour but very serious.

134

Madison opened her mouth, arms folded – but then she shut it again and sniffed. 'Yeah. No one's blaming you.'

'It was an accident,' said Nishat.

'Could've been any of us,' said Halid.

'Especially you, you muppet,' said Alfie.

They had a friendly little scuffle on the steps, while Big Mohammad gave Efe a tissue from his pocket.

'Sucks that we never got to set nothing on fire, though,' said Alfie sadly, kicking the metal bin.

All of 7E nodded and sighed at the lost opportunity to burn things.

'Wait!' said Billie, turning round to look at the steps and the three NutriGenix bottles. 'Where are all the secrets?'

All of 7E stared around too. We searched the bushes. We looked in the big recycling bin. But no one found it.

The shiny green ball of secrets had *vanished*.

JEM

Dear Miss Eagle,

Get well soon. Don't worry about the secrets. We'll fix it. I'm going to use magic, and the others are going to do boring detective stuff like asking who has it and checking the CCTV. I bet my way will be quickest. I can tell these things, Miss Eagle.

Broken ankles look disgusting, it turns out. I hope you didn't look at it. I would feel sick for ever if I had seen my own leg looking that disgusting.

Also, everyone is totally worrying about the play now - except for me, because messing with pain-in-the-bum fairies is probably what made you fall off the step. Just saying.

From Jemima Magee, aged 11¼

Afterwards we all went to Billie's café, which was my idea.

'Why *were* you in Mrs Cooper's office, Efe?' I asked.

She huddled in her long coat. 'No reason,' she whispered.

'Never mind about that!' said Sam. 'What about all the secrets?'

Efe shrank even further inside her coat. 'What if it's lost for ever?' she sniffled.

'Maybe a teacher took it,' said Billie. 'For safekeeping.'

'Maybe the paramedics picked it up in case it was her handbag,' said Georgie.

'That would be a pretty weird handbag,' said Billie, sucking Coke through a straw.

'She was going to burn it anyway,' I said. 'And now it's probably in a bin, all squished under banana skins and chocolate wrappers, which is practically the same thing. I don't know why you're all so stressed out.'

'It's all right for you,' snapped Billie. 'You didn't put a secret in.'

I thought about telling them the truth – but I quite liked being special and not like them too. Anyway, when your secret is a witchy secret, you have to be very careful with it. You can't go telling just anyone, or the magic might unravel, and then everything would be terrible.

But I could see Georgie's knees jiggling about under the table, all panicky.

So instead I promised to do a spell to help find it – which was totally nice of me, actually – only Billie scrunched up her nose at that too.

'We're only doing sensible, practical, proper things that are actually going to help,' she said. 'Not made-up kid stuff. This is *serious*.'

I waited for Sam to correct her, because if Sam didn't believe in magic, then she shouldn't have been eating two spoonfuls of it per day. But she didn't. Georgie didn't, either. And Efe just sniffled into her straw, wiping her red eyes.

'I'm going home,' I said, standing up, because that was where I could properly do something practical to help.

I waited, my coat on and my bag on my shoulder, and I did our special cough, which is three short coughs in a row and means, *Let's go now, please*. We made it up when we were eight.

But Georgie didn't get up. 'I haven't finished my Coke,' she whispered, clutching the can so hard it crinkled.

She could have picked it up and brought it with her. That is the whole point of having a can of Coke and not a glass of Coke.

But I didn't want to point that out and make her look stupid, so I said, 'No, you stay, Georgie. I'm really glad you're making friends – I know you're not usually very good at that,' and I went home by myself.

I was only saying what was true. No one could be upset about that.

It was lucky I came back by myself anyway – because when I got home, I could hear Tilly and Noah fighting in the office, in front of Mina's laptop.

'Not that one! That one isn't anything like it!'

'But it's pretty!'

'It's too different! Everyone will know!'

'Everyone will know what?' I said loudly, lowering my school bag carefully to the floor.

'Aaargh!' yelled Tilly, slamming the laptop closed with a bang.

'Ow!' yelped Noah, whose fingers were still on the keyboard and were now squashed flat.

'Sorry!' yelled Tilly, opening it again so he could suck on them – and revealing a photo of a huge and ancient ostrich egg.

It was for sale on an auction website, for bids beginning at twenty-five pounds.

My heart did a sad little backflip.

'Oh, you *didn't*,' I said, even though I knew they did.

'It's not my fault!' said Tilly.

'Or mine!' said Noah.

'It is totally your fault – shush,' said Tilly. 'It was Noah who took the egg. I'm just helping him fix it, because that is what big sisters do.'

My heart did another little backflip.

'I didn't mean to hurt it,' said Noah in a quavery voice. 'I wanted to grow an ostrich. A baby one. So I took the egg and I put it in lots of fluffy white towels and warm blankets, like the nest we made for Spooky on New Year's Eve, and then I sat on it so it would get warm and think there was a mummy ostrich sitting on it and get borned. Only . . .'

He reached across the desk and pulled a small brown paper bag towards him.

Inside it were the pale cracked shards of the broken ostrich egg, jumbled together like an impossible jigsaw.

'It turned out there wasn't a baby ostrich in there anyway,' said Tilly.

'It was all hollow. So it squashed.'

They both looked ever so sad and sorry. I think it must be dead hard being a teacher or a dad or a mum and telling people off all the time, when everyone looks ever so sad and sorry.

'Why did you pretend it was Janusz? Why didn't you just tell me, Nono?'

''Cos you'd have told Georgie.'

'And she'd have told Mina,' said Tilly.

'And then we'd be definitely in great big huge trouble,' said Noah.

'So I thought we could buy a new one and put it where the other egg was, and no one would ever need to know. Only they cost loads, and I spent all my money on love.'

'We're going to save up, though, and then we can buy a whole new egg and Mina won't be upset.' Noah stood up and hugged me round my middle. 'Please don't tell, Jem-Jem. Pleeeease.'

'Pleeeeeease,' said Tilly, clutching her hands together.

They were right, probably. I would definitely have told Georgie. And she would definitely have told her mum. But then I thought about Tilly saying she wanted to fix it because that is what big sisters do, and I knew Georgie would think so too, and feel all complicated and upset, and I knew I wouldn't tell.

I promised.

Then I went upstairs and unpacked my school bag very carefully, and changed into the skirt that Sam's mum had said was lovely even though it had holes and bunchiness.

I thought about the shiny green ball of secrets, and all the precious things hidden inside.

I thought about the cracked eggshell in its secret paper bag.

I thought about all the worried faces in the café, and the ever-so-sad and sorry ones downstairs.

And then I thought: *I don't think I will fix what happened today with magic.*

I decided to fix it with something else. Something secret, all my own.

GEORGIE

Jem and I spent all Friday evening making two cards.

One for Miss Eagle, with a drawing of Puck from *A Midsummer Night's Dream* bringing her a cup of tea in her hospital bed, to say sorry about her broken ankle.

And one for Mum, for her birthday. It had a rabbit on it, wearing a ribbon. We always got rabbit cards for each other, ever since it was just us two.

'If I help colour it in, can I put my name inside too?' asked Tilly. 'Because I sort of need my pocket money for other things that aren't birthday cards. Or presents.'

'And me,' said Noah.

I liked my card the way it was. I'd spent a long time drawing the rabbit ears and rubbing them out and drawing them again so they were just right. But it seemed the sort of thing big sisters ought to do, so I said yes.

Tilly fetched paintbrushes and squirty paint. By the time they were finished the card was wet and drooping under the weight of the now-invisible rabbit's outfit. It was still sticky and sodden on Saturday morning, when we took a tray upstairs to their bedroom with tea and marmalade toast.

We always did birthdays on Mum's bed too. It felt a bit crowded, having four other people and a cat there.

'Well, how charming,' said Mum, not touching the card when Noah thrust it towards her. 'Why don't you put it somewhere to dry? Like, outside in the garden?'

I gave her a new pen in a fancy box with red velvet lining.

'Beautiful,' she said, kissing my nose.

Jem gave her chocolates, which she sighed at and put in a drawer.

Then Joel slid an envelope across the breakfast table. 'Nothing too grand,' he said shyly.

Mum opened it, pulled out a few pieces of brightly printed card – and screamed.

'You did *not*!'

'I did *so*,' said Joel.

'*How* did you?! *How?* These were impossible to get . . . I tried and tried . . . I called everyone I know . . . I got Martin to phone up and pretend to be related to the Duchess of Cambridge . . .!' She flung herself into Joel's arms like it was the end of a soppy film, and kissed him very hard on the lips.

'I love you,' she said.

'I love you too, Minkydink.'

'You're my absolute favourite in the whole wide world.'

'You're my favourite, all the way out into space.'

'You're my favourite to the scientific limits of the measurable cosmos, and a little bit further—'

Jem made a vomity noise, which I couldn't help agreeing with, even though, obviously, people being in love is very nice. Meanwhile Tilly was furiously taking notes.

'Look, darling! Can you believe it?' said Mum, flapping them under my nose: two tickets to see Ekaterina Yashvilinova dancing in *Swan Lake*. Tonight.

'Oh!' I squeaked, understanding at once.

Ekaterina Yashvilinova was our favourite ballerina. We had DVDs of all her performances. I'd watched her since I was tiny. The tickets for the *Swan Lake* tour had gone on sale months and months ago, and had sold out in minutes. Mum had been in tears. I'd been in tears. She'd called everyone she knew, and none of them had tickets, either. They were literally like gold dust – except for apparently being printed card with logos on once you actually managed to get hold of them.

'They aren't brilliant seats,' said Joel, still looking pretty pleased with himself. 'And they still cost a packet. But I was chatting with Steve-o at work – about you, Georgie, and all your dancing – and he said his ex had won this pricey pair of tickets to this ballet-show thingamajig that everyone and his dog wanted to go to, and now they weren't going on account of him being his ex now, so . . . I wasn't going to say no, right?'

I beamed up at Mum and gave her a tight hug. I couldn't believe it. We were actually going, like we'd dreamed about and had to give up on. It was the best present, the most wonderful present . . . I'd been so worried about my lost secret in the green ball, and now here was this wonderful, magical thing to make it all disappear . . .

I gave Joel a tight hug too. I couldn't help it. He looked very surprised – but then he hugged back gently and pressed his big hand on the back of my head, and I didn't mind. I liked it.

Jem hopped off the bed, saying, 'Come on! Mum'll be here to pick us up in ten minutes' – and Mum's hands flew to her lips.

'Oh! But – it's *tonight*! And – if they're all going off to see Bridget . . . what are we going to do with Georgie? She can't stay in the house all by herself.'

'But I won't be,' I said. 'I'll be going with you.'

As soon as it came out of my mouth, I realized.

The tickets weren't for me and Mum.

The tickets were for Mum and Joel.

The happy couple.

Each other's favourite.

Mum's mouth went thin. Joel looked horrified.

'There were only two tickets . . .' he mumbled. 'Only two, anywhere . . . I wasn't meaning to . . . It was more like . . .'

'A romantic thing,' I said in a very quiet voice.

'Oh, Georgiepoo,' said Mum.

And that made it a hundred times worse. It made me feel like a little girl; only a little girl would think her mummy wanted to go to the ballet with her daughter and not her boyfriend.

'I didn't think,' said Joel, looking imploringly at Jem as if she could help. 'I just thought, the kids'll be at Bridgie's, so . . .'

'Da-ad,' said Jem, glaring, because she understood that made it even worse. I wasn't one of the kids. He'd forgotten all about me.

'It's fine,' I said stiffly, straightening my shoulders like Miss Adjoa always told me to at the start of a performance. 'You two go and have a lovely time. Spooky will be here to keep me company.' Spooky chose that moment to leap off the bed in apparent disgust. 'Or – or I'll just be by myself. It'll be fine. It's only till you get back home after it finishes.'

Mum and Joel exchanged guilty looks.

'It's in Cardiff, darling, not London.'

'I booked us a hotel. Treat, with my first pay packet,' said Joel guiltily.

Mum gripped the tickets tightly. 'We won't go. We'll give them to someone else. It'll be fine.

Unless . . .' She raised one eyebrow, looking from Joel to Jem to Joel again. 'You don't suppose . . . I mean, we are all one big family now . . .'

'You mean . . .?' said Jem.

'Georgie goes with them on their visitation weekend with their ma?' said Joel, blinking.

'Can she? Can she, Dad? Can you?' squeaked Tilly, gripping the duvet.

'Pleeeease,' said Noah, clinging onto my leg. 'It's mean, leaving you behind. Mum said so last week.'

'Did she now?' said Mum.

'Um,' said Jem, which meant she had.

I felt a little rush of hope and warmth.

Joel hopped out of bed. When he came back, he was smiling. 'All sorted. She's, uh, running late, as it happens, but she'll scoot along this afternoon and pick you all up. Pack a sleeping bag, Georgie? And she'll pop you all back home on Sunday afternoon. Treat for all of us, eh?'

I was still sad about Ekaterina Yashvilinova and *Swan Lake*, and not being Mum's favourite, but I pushed the feeling away. I was wanted somewhere else. I was going to Jem's mum's flat, all the way to Croydon, like a Magee. Like I was part of that family too.

'Treat for all of us,' I said, squeezing Jem's hand.

'Yeah,' she said. Then she let go, and fussed around with the packing, and went to sit on her window seat all by herself.

JEM

Dear Dad,

We all like the way you are super good at presents, like the time you got me unicorn things that year I was really into unicorns, and now getting Mina this ballet thing. Only next time maybe remember you have more than three children now because it is pretty rude to forget.

Also, you could check with me if it is OK for Georgie to come, not just with Mum and Tilly and Noah.

I don't mind sharing you. I mind sharing Mum, a bit. I already have to share her with her invisible secret man-friend and there's, like, half an arm left after that.

Some love from Jemima Magee, aged 11¼

I knew Georgie could tell I was cross because she went all mouse-like in the car on the way to Croydon.

I didn't mean to be cross. I could feel me doing it and I knew it was mean. It's just hard to stop, once you are.

And her being a mouse didn't help at all. Mum doesn't understand shyness. She thinks it's rude stuck-upness instead.

'There you go, Georgie – squish up in between the car seats, that's it. Now, let's have a look at you. Teeth? Ears? Shoes all done up?'

Georgie didn't giggle and pull down her lips or wave her legs in the air with the rest of us. She sat stiff like a doll, with her seat belt done up and her hands all neat in her lap.

Mum narrowed her eyes. 'No fancy hairdos today, Nono?'

'Georgie didn't have time,' he said sadly.

'She had to do her violin practice and her dancing practice instead,' said Tilly.

'Of course she did,' said Mum. Her mouth twitched at the corner.

Then she turned to me in the front seat, gave me a secret little look and drove off.

153

I smiled back; I like it when me and Mum have secret little front-seat things, just between us witches. She was wearing her patchouli perfume again, and her favourite coat: the green-and-purple-patchwork one that has tiny round mirrors sewn all over it. I was glad I'd worn my patchwork skirt so we were matchy.

But then I looked back and saw Georgie twisting her hands in her lap, and felt rotten.

It was the same for the rest of the day.

We went to the park, and Georgie wouldn't play frisbee golf because she was worried about breaking her ankle.

('She'll twirl about in a tutu all morning,' said Mum, flinging a ball at Tilly's head, 'but now it's actual fun she's got to have a wee rest?')

We went to McDonald's, and Georgie wouldn't have anything because Mina didn't believe in McDonald's.

('It's not a figment of my imagination, sweetheart,' said Mum, knocking on the plastic table with her knuckles. 'Trust me, if I'd dreamed it up, a Large Fries would be a whole lot larger, and a Happy Meal would actually make you happy. Guaranteed or your money back.')

We went back to the flat to watch *Inside Out* with a tub of chocolate ice cream, and Georgie went off to sit at the kitchen counter and read her Shakespeare book by herself.

('Does she know it's not Sunday night?' said Mum, licking her spoon. 'Who does their homework before last thing Sunday night?')

She wasn't even reading properly. I could see her eyes darting around, noting all the things in the flat that Mina wouldn't ever have in our house: the crystals on the edge of the TV table; the phases-of-the-moon mobile that hung by the front door; joss sticks sending out little curls of smoke and the smell of violet and jasmine.

When it got to bedtime for Tilly and Noah, me and Mum pulled out the sofa bed together, and made up an extra bed on the side out of cushions wrapped in a sheet, just for Georgie. I laid her sleeping bag on top. Georgie had disappeared off to the bathroom. When she came back, she was wearing her best pyjamas: satiny purple trousers and a floaty white top with spotty purple ribbons in bows that tied at the shoulder. They were really nice, I thought. They were much nicer than my pyjamas, which were Dad's cut-off old jogging bottoms and a red T-shirt with a hole in one armpit. I wouldn't have minded having pyjamas like those. But I knew that Mum would think they were show-offy. I could see her pressing her lips together as she fetched a pillow for Georgie's bed.

Then Georgie said, 'Thank you for having me, Mrs Magee,' and put out her hand for Mum to shake.

It was too much. Mum let out a snort and clutched a pillow to her face; then her big laugh rang out like a bell. Tilly and Noah both wriggled under the bedcovers to giggle. I put a hand over my mouth and tried really, really hard not to join in, but my tummy jiggled to give me away.

Georgie let out a huge sniff, then fled back into the bathroom and locked the door.

'Mum!' I said.

She looked at me, distraught but still giggling. 'I just— Sorry, baby. Couldn't help myself. A handshake! She's ever so sweet, love – but, oh, for a kid she makes a grand little old woman.'

I glared at her. I kicked the covers until the giggling stopped and two heads peeped out.

'You're all mean,' I said. 'Now go to sleep – and *you*, go to bed – and tomorrow you'd better be much nicer, and not ever say anything about it at all, ever. OK?'

'OK,' they all mumbled.

I went to the bathroom and listened to the shuddery sound of Georgie crying in big gulpy sobs. I gave the door a guilty tap. 'It's only me,' I whispered. 'The others have all gone to bed. Can I come in? I won't be mean. I'll be nice, I promise.'

There was a lot of sniffing. Then, with a click, the door unlocked and opened a crack.

Inside, Georgie was sitting on the toilet lid, clutching mounds of soggy toilet paper, her face all streaky and red.

'I tried so hard, all afternoon!' she gulped out. 'I was excited to come, but then I could see you didn't want me here, so I tried to keep out of the way and not be a bother, and let you have your special time with your mum like I wasn't even here at all. But that wasn't right, either. Saying thank you wasn't right. I can't do anything right at all!'

I felt awful then. I'd thought she was just being annoying and weird for no reason, when instead she was being annoying and weird while trying to be kind. I should've guessed. It was a very Georgie thing to do.

So I gave her a big tight hug and let her cry on my T-shirt for a bit.

Then I said, 'I'm really sorry for being mean and cross and a bit like I didn't want you to come.'

'It's OK,' she sniffed. 'I wouldn't want me, either.'

I thought for a bit. 'Maybe you and my mum should spend more time together. Then she wouldn't think you were stuck up, and you wouldn't think she didn't like you – because obviously once she knows you properly she'll like you loads.'

Georgie looked at me. 'Does she think I'm stuck up?'

'Yeah. And she thinks your mum has too much money, and that's why Dad likes her best.'

Georgie frowned. 'You aren't supposed to talk about how much money you've got – it's rude.'

'See? My mum would say you only care about that if you've got loads. My mum thinks you should talk about *everything*.'

There was a knuckly tap on the door, and Mum peeped in. Her hair was damp round her clean face, and she was wearing a nightie with sugar skulls on it.

'I can't sleep, leaving you like this. I'm sorry, Georgie. Can you forgive me? I'm not always very good at being an adult.'

Georgie nodded, her eyes big. 'I don't think I'm very good at being a person at all,' she whispered.

Mum put her hand on her heart. 'Oh, sweetheart. Hugs?'

They did hugs. I wanted one too, but I was good and sat on the toilet lid instead, because not everything is about me. Dad says.

'Now then, miss – are you hungry? You've eaten like a bird today while we've all been stuffing ourselves. There's one fifth of a tub of chocolate ice cream out there with your name on. We saved it for you.'

I bit my lip – I knew that Mina would have said, *Ice cream, just before bed? I don't think so, darling.*

But Georgie nodded her head at once. 'Yes, please. That's ever so kind of you.' Then she clapped a hand over her mouth in horror – till Mum laughed her big laugh and gave her a nudge.

'We could all learn some manners off this one, eh?'

'*I* say please!' I protested. 'Sometimes.'

We took the ice cream back to Mum's bedroom with three spoons, and had a pyjama party sitting on her bed, just us three.

'Come on then, girls. I want all the gossip from school.'

'Well,' I said. 'Miss Eagle fell off a step. And we all saw her boobies.'

'Only a little bit! Of one boobie!' said Georgie. 'Billie covered her up. And she broke her ankle. Miss Eagle, not Billie. She went off in an ambulance. And Big Mohammad gave Efe a hug in front of the whole class, even though she's only a four-out-of-ten and he's an eight.'

'Well now,' said Mum.

'And someone stole my carrot sticks out of my lunch box,' Georgie went on, her hands starting to move as she talked. 'Which made me really cross – although it was much worse for Sam because her whole hummus wrap got eaten. And Halid read out Nishat's diary, which was awful, though now Acacia is really careful not to throw netballs at her face any more – I watched her in PE. And now all the secrets from our secret ball of secrets have gone missing, and we don't know where they went or if anyone's read them.'

'Oh!' said Mum. She nudged me, grinning. 'I thought you said this one was shy?'

Georgie blushed. 'And – and we probably won't be able to do the play after all without Miss Eagle, and I'll never find out if I could've been a brave fairy dancing in front of everyone.'

'Now, we can't have that! The show must go on!' said Mum, leaning forward, all involved. 'Tell me about this play, my love. I did a wee bit of acting myself – you know, back when I was at school . . .'

Georgie fetched the big Shakespeare book, and they curled up together. Which was brilliant, actually, because I was a bit sick of ice cream anyway.

FEBRUARY

GEORGIE

It did not turn out to be good news for Miss Eagle.

'Dislocated, and broken in two places,' said Mr Miller. 'Needed an operation. Two pins to hold it all together. She'll be in plaster for weeks. Off school for months.' He looked almost perky about it – or at least a lot less sleepy than usual.

'Yeah, but how is she, sir?' asked Big Mohammad.

'When will she be back?' asked Nishat.

'Does it still hurt?' asked Efe in a tiny voice.

Mr Miller leaned back in his chair. 'Oh, she's doing all right – lots of painkillers. I was the first member of staff to visit, you know,' he said, puffing out his chest. 'Mrs Cooper hasn't been in. Sent a card, apparently. I took flowers. And grapes. And a ball of wool. Eleanor loves knitting . . .'

'Do you fancy her, sir?' said Madison.

'Are you her boyfriend, sir?' called Lianne.

I expected Mr Miller to tell them to shush – but instead he got a very smirky look on his face and stroked his cardigan buttons.

'Ew,' said Sam, wrinkling up her nose.

I hated asking questions in class, but I put my hand up anyway. I needed to know. 'Did she have the post box with her, sir? The green ball with all the secrets in it?'

I could feel the nervous hope in the room.

But Mr Miller shook his head. 'Eh? Nope. Didn't see anything like that.' He sighed. 'I expect she'll need a lift home from the hospital. You can guarantee no one else'll offer . . . She'll see who her real friends are, just you wait . . .'

Then he got Billie to take the register while he twirled round and round on his desk chair, humming.

'Poor Miss Eagle,' said Billie at lunch time.

'Yeah,' said Sam, sighing at the empty space in her lunch box where her apple used to be. 'Imagine having to go out with Mr Miller. Urgh.'

'Never mind about him,' said Billie crossly. 'What about the play? Who's going to do Shakespeare with us if Miss Eagle's off for months?'

For our English lesson that morning we'd had a very boring supply teacher, who made us all sit in silence and read copies of *Treasure Island*, one between two.

'Well,' I said quietly. 'Actually I had an idea about that.'

'Did you?' said Jem.

I felt my face hot up because I don't usually have ideas by myself. But Jem had been grumpy ever since Bridget drove us home two hours early on Sunday. I knew why: there must be a date happening with the invisible secret man-friend. I'd already offered to help out with wiping all the eyeliner off the pillows when whoever-he-was stopped being nice and sexy-faced, but that didn't cheer her up at all; she'd spent all afternoon brewing something secret in the kitchen, which smelled of raw onions and was allegedly 'Man-friend Repellent'. ('Reckon it's everything repellent, love,' said Joel that evening, when no one would sit in there for dinner.)

'Yes,' I said. 'Or – it was your mum's idea, kind of. You'd already fallen asleep when she thought of it. I told her all about Miss Eagle and the play, and how we wouldn't be able to do it any more, and she said – she thought – she thinks we could just do it ourselves.'

Bridget thought I had Hidden Depths too. I'd told her all about the play Mum took me to in Regent's Park. When I'd shown her the dance steps that I half remembered, she said it absolutely *had* to happen.

'Ooh,' said Billie.

'As a sort of tribute to Miss Eagle being a nice teacher?' said Sam.

'And to show how sorry we are about her broken ankle?' whispered Efe.

'Yes! And I thought we could do it at the Easter Extravaganza, just like she planned. She'll be well enough to come and watch by then. It could be a secret sort of surprise.' I looked awkwardly at Jem. 'I didn't mean to leave you out. It's just . . . not really your sort of thing.'

Jem sniffed. 'No fear. Anyway, I have a lot of other things to do.'

'Do *I* have to be in it? Like, in front of everyone?' whispered Efe.

Sam looked thoughtful. 'There's always behind-the-scenes things with plays. Like hammering and stuff. Right, Georgie?'

I nodded.

'I will do hammering,' whispered Efe.

'We need a name,' said Billie. 'To make it sound official.'

'I thought so too,' I said, feeling shy again suddenly. 'Um. I thought we could be Miss Eagle's Emergency Extravaganzers. Or MEEE, for short.'

'I love it,' said Billie, her eyes sparkling.

We made a list of all the characters we needed, and a list of everyone in 7E, so we could start recruiting right away.

By the end of lunch I thought perhaps I wouldn't be a dancer when I grew up. I might be a director of a theatre, because it turned out that if it was something I cared about, and knew about, and knew better than anyone, I really liked telling people what to do.

I couldn't wait to go home and tell Mum all about it.

But before I had the chance, something much more enormous happened.

It started in our German lesson. Mr Nevins unrolled a big poster about *Das Campingplatz*. But instead of lots of *Schlafsäcke* and *Taschenlampen*, all we noticed was the slip of yellow paper stuck on the front, which said in biro capitals:

MISS EAGLE IS FIT AND I WOULD LIKE TO TOUCH HER ON THE BUM.

We all gasped.

'Oh my days, that is *totally* one of the secrets,' said Madison.

'Out of that green ball, innit,' said Lianne.

'It can't be,' said Nishat, looking sick.

I felt a horrible airless feeling in my chest.

Jem bit her lip and held my hand; she knew just what I was thinking.

'That ain't even a secret, bruv,' said Big Mohammad. 'Everyone knows Miss Eagle is fit.'

'Well fit,' agreed Alfie.

'Mmmm,' said Halid in a weirdly strangly squeak.

Big Mohammad and Alfie spun round in their chairs to stare at him. Then we all did.

'What?' murmured Halid shiftily.

'No way, bruv,' said Alfie, prodding him on the arm.

'That is you, bruv,' said Big Mohammad. 'That is, like, your secret for definites.'

Halid squirmed in his seat in a way that kind of said *YES* to the whole room.

'Look! There's another one! Stuck to the window!' said Billie, suddenly standing up and pointing.

I am the lunch-box thief.

'Yes, all right, sit down, please,' said Mr Nevins crossly, pulling down the secret and crumpling it up on his desk. 'Now, everyone turn to page *zweiundfünfzig* . . .'

But it was hard to concentrate on page fifty-two when we kept finding more secrets stuck up

171

all over the room, making me hold my breath every time.

I murdered my goldfish on purpose so my mum would buy me a compensatory hamster, only it turns out hamsters are boring and always asleep.

I WISH I WAS SKINNY, BUT CURLY FRIES ARE THE ONLY THINGS THAT MAKE ME HAPPY.

I am not really French at all – I am just pretending so I don't have to talk to anyone.

'*Bof?*' said Ariadne Ocean Dupree feebly.

'No way!' said Alfie, his mouth dropping open.

Ariadne Ocean Dupree sighed, her shoulders drooping. 'OK. I suppose there isn't much point pretending any more. Wow. This is weird. Um. Hi, everyone?'

She turned out to have a thick Scottish accent, and to be perfectly able to speak English.

'I wish I'd thought of that,' sighed Sam. 'No one even tries to give her homework.'

That day Mr Nevins gave us *all* homework.

The next secret was found on the smartboard in Mrs Ling's Science lab.

> I stole Nishat's diary and put it in that book but I only did it 'cos Nishat got more out of ten than Madison, which was well unfair.

'Oh my days,' said Lianne loudly, and dropped three test tubes of potassium sulphate in shock.

'Good heavens!' said Mrs Ling.

'You never!' shouted Madison. 'I was the one that wrote those lists! And I had to give myself only, like, six out of ten, so I didn't look all big-headed!'

'Oh my days!' shouted Lianne. 'You gave me like nine out of ten – that is well sweet!'

'I know, right?' shouted Madison. And they hugged next to all the broken glass, and apparently forgot all about poor Nishat, and –22 Edmond Hudson, and the new girl who had been called fat.

Seven E trooped very nervously to our next lesson, Maths.

Sure enough, Billie found more secrets on slips of paper – this time tucked into an old coffee mug on Mrs Cox-Patel's desk, much to her surprise. But none of them were mine.

I am a secret chess wizard.

I've never kissed anyone. (Yet)

I am really very afraid of bees, miss.

I HAVE ACROPHOBIA. THAT MEANS I AM VERY AFRAID OF HEIGHTS. BUT I AM SOMETIMES QUITE BRAVE ABOUT IT. PLEASE DON'T TELL ANYONE. FROM SAM (THE BOY ONE)

'You muppet!' said Sam. 'You weren't supposed to sign it!'

'It was going to get burned,' the boy Sam mumbled.

'It's OK,' said Nishat comfortingly. 'Everyone already knows you're scared of heights.'

Then Alfie found another one taped to the window.

> I really like having a twin brother. He used to hang around with me more because of being pathetic and friendless, and I kind of miss him now he's always at art club. (DON'T TELL ANYONE.)

Sam looked sheepish. 'There are probably loads of people with twin brothers around,' she muttered.

'Aw,' said the boy Sam, his freckly face turning pink. 'I love you too.'

'I said *like*! *Like!*' yelled Sam, and punched him on the arm.

'Yeah, yeah,' said the boy Sam, rubbing it.

*

175

The last lesson of the day was History. I didn't hear a word of what Mrs Lewis said about Roman roads. I kept eyeing the walls, and the windows, and the mug on her desk, waiting.

When the bell rang, Jem had to prod me to get me out of my chair.

'I can't believe it,' whispered Efe on the way to the gates. 'All our secrets . . .'

'Who could be doing it?' asked Jem, looking around warily at the rest of the students pouring out of school.

'Um. Yeah. I was wondering that too,' said Billie, scratching her ear nervously.

But I didn't care who or why.

I just wanted to know *when*.

When *my* secret would appear on the wall, and crumble everything happy away.

JEM

Dear Miss Eagle,
   I hope you didn't read all the secrets in the ball. Especially that one about Halid touching your bum.
   And even more especially not mine. Or Georgie's.
   Also I don't really like English or lessons, and I never cared all that much about your play thing, but it turns out Georgie does, like, a lot. Also nothing is worse than reading 'Treasure Island' one between two. Basically, hurry up and mend your leg soon. Please.

From Jemima Magee, aged 11¼

When we got home, Georgie went straight upstairs and shut her bedroom door.

I tapped on it a few times, but she shouted, 'I'm doing my violin practice!' in a high squeaky voice, even though there weren't any violin noises coming out.

I felt awful for five minutes. Then I knew just what to do.

I went to find Tilly – who was adding a cemetery made of matchbox gravestones to the rear of her cardboard doll's house – and Noah, who was teaching the Morrises to sing *We Wish You a Merry Christmas*, which is the only song he knows all the words to.

'Superglue,' I whispered.

They both jumped up at once.

We gathered in the kitchen.

'I brought Maurice Morris to help,' said Noah, putting Maurice the mouse on the table.

'I brought actual glue,' said Tilly, producing the pot, although most of it seemed to be smeared on her school skirt. 'What are we fixing?'

'Georgie,' I said. 'She's got the sads.'

The sads is what you get when you're poorly with miserableness, instead of with itchy spots like chicken pox or with a broken leg if you're a giraffe. Dad had it loads after Mum left.

Tilly and Noah both put their hands over their mouths.

'Should we tell Mina?' asked Tilly, looking anxious.

Mina was working from home today, locked in her office with a DO NOT DISTURB sign dangling from the door handle on a golden chain.

I shook my head. 'She's probably selling important Fairy Dusters things to China or something. Anyway, we can manage.'

First I found Dad's old cookery book with the recipe for oaty biscuits in it, because biscuits make everyone feel cheerful. We had everything we needed except for golden syrup, so we made our own out of sugar and water with some lemon squash in it 'to make it goldener', according to Noah.

'What else does Georgie like?' he asked.

'Dancing,' I said. 'Especially ballet. And music. And books, and seriousness, and frog jokes. And me.'

'And nice piley-up hairdos,' Tilly reminded me. 'This is going to be dead easy.'

Two hours later, when Dad came home, he found, pinned to the door, a poster made of pink sugar paper with glued-on jewels and heavy felt pen.

ROLL UP! ROLL UP!
ONE NIGHT ONLY!
COME AND SEE
THE BALLET OF GEORGIE AND JEM AND A FROG
IN THE BACK ROOM
TICKETS £2.50

Inside, a roll of paper made a red carpet leading to the back room. The blue sofa had been pushed round to face the fireplace, which was now a stage flanked by armchairs, with a sheet draped across to form a curtain.

'This is nothing to do with me,' said Mina, throwing up her hands as I pulled her out of her office.

'We did our own make-up,' said Noah proudly, grinning and revealing lipsticky teeth.

'And costumes,' said Tilly, who was wearing my bunchy skirt and a top made of a Tesco bag with holes cut in. They both had their hair up on top of their heads in big pineapples.

'I can see that, lads,' said Dad, pulling off his uniform tie and his name badge.

'Two pounds fifty, please,' Tilly demanded, putting out her hand.

'I thought the thieves were all back at work!' he said. 'Go on then. Two, please.'

Tilly took his five-pound note and beamed at Noah as she led them both to the sofa.

I went upstairs to fetch Georgie.

She didn't answer when I tapped on the door, but I opened it anyway. She was lying on her bed, quite covered in sads.

'We made you a thing,' I said, kneeling next to her. 'And I promise it will make you feel better.'

'Are you sure?' she said in a small voice.

'One hundred per cent guaranteed.'

'You don't have to pay because your name is in the title, and that's the rules,' said Noah when she came downstairs.

The Ballet of Georgie and Jem and a Frog was not really a ballet, except for Noah wearing Georgie's pale blue leotard and white ballet shoes over his school uniform, hopping about a lot with his arms over his head while we played Mina's *Swan Lake* CD in the background. Tilly refused to do anything approaching a dance, and read all her lines off her arm in a shouty voice. I spent the show hiding behind one of the armchairs, doing the voice of the Frog (as played by Horace Morris the brontosaurus). But everyone seemed to be enjoying it.

The story was all about Georgie and me meeting in the playground when we were eight – except this time we met a magic frog (or brontosaurus), and it took us on adventures to magical lands, like in *The Magic Faraway Tree*, while telling jokes out of a joke book. We went to a land made entirely of cheese, and one where everything was upside down (which involved a lot of wobbly handstands), and another where it was really dark all the time (we turned off the lights).

'And now it is time for the interval!' shouted Tilly, flicking the lights back on.

They fetched the oaty biscuits, which had turned out very thin and crispy, with black frills round the edges and a strong taste of washing-up liquid.

'One pound, please!' said Tilly, sticking out her hand again.

'Well, this is all very entrepreneurial,' said Mina as Dad sighed and handed over coins from his pocket.

'It's for a good cause,' said Noah darkly.

'Yours is free because you are a special guest,' Tilly told Georgie.

'We didn't even lick it,' added Noah.

'Thank you,' said Georgie, giving me a bewildered look.

We all had a biscuit, and then a glass of water to take the taste away.

The second half was not as successful. My book ran out of frog jokes. Tilly went to the toilet and accidentally washed all her lines off her arm. Noah fell over Spooky, who had decided he didn't like being left out and ran on stage to bite the curtains. Mina kept looking at her watch and making whispery noises.

'Skip to the end, skip to the end!' I hissed from behind the armchair.

'What happens at the end?' asked Noah.

I jumped out from behind the armchair and declared, 'Look! I was not a frog-slash-brontosaurus all along! I am your fairy godmother!'

'Ooh!' said Tilly and Noah.

'With a wave of my wand – which I have left behind the armchair so I will use this,' I said, improvising and plucking a glittery twig out of the nearest vase. 'With this superglue I make you sisters for ever, so you will never be lonely again! *Swoosh!*'

I threw lots of torn-up bits of paper in the air.

'Yaaaay!' yelled Tilly and Noah, dancing around in a circle.

Then they sang *We Wish You a Merry Christmas*, but with new words that said, *We all really like Georgie*, over and over again.

'Oh,' said Georgie. 'Gosh. Um.' And then she burst into tears.

'Oh no!' said Noah, wrapping his arms round her leg.

'Darling, are you all right?' said Mina, holding her hand.

'Yes!' squeaked Georgie from underneath Tilly's pineapple hair as she joined in the hugging. 'Happy tears. Nice. Um. Thank you.'

'Grand job, lads,' said Dad, clapping loudly. 'Worth every penny. I'll get the hoover.'

He caught my eye, jerking his head towards the hallway.

'Hey. Did something happen at school today?' he asked in a low voice, once we were alone.

'Um. Sort of. But it's fine. We're fixing it.'

'Uh-huh,' said Dad, looking unconvinced. 'You know, you don't have to do that all by yourself, kid. You can ask for help.'

'I've got help, duh,' I said.

Then I went to wash the lipstick off all the places where Noah had put his face.

We had pizza for dinner. Mina ate one very small piece very slowly, with lots of frondy lettuce. Georgie hardly had any, either.

It was my turn to help wash up, and when I was finished I went to find her – but she wasn't in her bedroom. Eventually I found her sitting on the bench in the garden, wrapped in her coat and her polar-bear hat, swinging her legs.

'Did we make you feel better?'

She nodded. 'You really did. It was a bit amazing, actually. But – oh, Jem, what if it keeps happening? What if *all* the secrets come out?'

She looked so pale and panicked my heart felt fizzy. I squeezed her hand tightly. 'Maybe they won't.'

'But what if they do?' She looked cross then. 'It's all right for you. You don't even have a secret. If you did, you'd want to find out who showed them to everyone and . . . and punch them in the ear. Twice. And get them arrested, or expelled, or put in a bin.'

I nearly told her, right away, that I had a secret too; one that I had slipped into that shiny green letter box. One I never wanted her to find out.

But I had a better idea.

'I suppose we could try to find out who it was,' I said slowly. 'But I've been thinking . . . I bet Miss

Eagle would like my idea. I bet she'd think it was even better than burning all the secrets.'

Georgie looked up hopefully.

'Those secrets – they're things people feel bad about, or scared about; things they're carrying around on their insides like a . . . a volcano, waiting to go off – *boom*.'

She nodded, eyes wide and sad. 'That's just how it feels,' she whispered.

I nodded too. 'And that's awful. So – we could run around finding out who is posting the secrets, yeah. But we could try to be more useful than that. Like, the goldfish-murdering person has got a hamster now. Why don't we help that hamster find a new home? Or give the curly-fries person something else to be happy about? Then the secrets get to do some good. And – and the volcano doesn't go *boom*. It stops being a volcano altogether. It's just an ordinary internal mountain-type thing instead.'

'Oh, Jem,' whispered Georgie. 'I like it. I like it a lot.'

'We could do it in secret. Just us two together. We should have a name as well. To make it official. The Secret Squad.'

'The SS?' Georgie's nose crinkled. 'Maybe not. Um . . . the Undercover Superglue Squad? Or USS for short.'

'USS for short,' I said happily. 'It's perfect.'

She hugged me on the bench.

'*Now* I feel better,' she said.

GEORGIE

I felt so much happier now I was in MEEE *and* in USS.

USS (i.e. me, in my notebook) had made a chart of the six secrets we'd seen so far but didn't know whose they were.

Lunch-box thief
Curly fries
Secret chess wizard
Never kissed anyone
Goldfish murderer
Scared of bees

We decided the goldfish murderer was the most urgent one to find – followed by the person who was only happy with curly fries. But we couldn't just ask – especially when everyone at school was as jumpy as Spooky near Janusz's vacuum cleaner.

Big Mohammad and Alfie had a fight in the playground about which of them had been standing nearest the green ball when Miss Eagle broke her ankle. Mrs Cox-Patel caused panic by casually brandishing a ruler that had something yellow stuck to it – but it was only an old Post-it note. 7E kept eyeing one other with deep suspicion.

Mrs Cooper held a special assembly just for Year 7s, all about how school was for learning and not for 'silly distractions'.

But I couldn't help being distracted; not when, under it all, there was the lingering fear that the rest of the secrets – *my* secret – would be stuck up next. I clung tightly to Jem every time we went into a new classroom.

Yet the next day, and the next, no more secrets appeared.

'It doesn't make sense,' said Sam at lunch time. 'Why not put them all up together?'

'Unless that *was* all the secrets.' Billie prodded a knot in the picnic table with a fingernail.

'Or . . . or maybe the person – the awful person – thought that some of the secrets were too secret to share.'

There was a nervous silence.

'Maybe some of them got lost,' said Efe. 'Because my secret did not get put on the wall. For definitely.' She tipped up her lunch-box lid, stuck her face inside and wouldn't look at anyone.

I had a small suspicion that perhaps this wasn't completely true, and shared a secret USS smile with Jem. Whatever it was, we'd make Efe's internal volcano turn into a mountain.

'At least the lunch-box thief's given up,' said Sam, opening her carrot sticks.

Then Billie opened her lunch box and lifted out a peeled banana, quite naked; this time the skin had disappeared. 'This is getting weird,' she said, putting it back, her face all crinkled up.

'My lunch is all gone,' said Jem, snapping her lunch box closed. 'See you later!' She threw me a wink.

'Er. Yes. Mine too. Better pop into the dining hall and see if they have any leftovers.' I hurried away before anyone could ask me anything.

At the end of lunch, me and Jem huddled on the steps to the sports complex together.

'I have sniffed everyone in Seven E, and none of them smell of hamsters,' said Jem sadly.

'I watched what everyone ate,' I said. 'Alfie, Halid and Nishat all had second helpings of curly fries. And it can't be Halid – he wants to touch Miss Eagle's bum.' I blushed when I said it.

'It can't be Alfie – he's got loads of friends,' said Jem. 'It's bound to be Nishat. She looks scared of everything.'

I could see what she meant. Nishat was very small and quiet, and had plaits like me – which didn't necessarily mean being scared of things, but it didn't not mean that, either.

'All we need now is to make her happy, then,' I said.

'I could make some more of the oaty biscuits,' suggested Jem.

The bell went before I could tell her I wasn't sure that would work, which was probably for the best.

*

After school Billie and Sam came home with us for a special planning meeting of MEEE.

I had planned to use the kitchen table to spread out all my careful directing notes – but Tilly and Noah had got there before us, and covered it completely with pink cardboard heart shapes, sequins, fluffy bobbles, pipe cleaners and glue.

'I asked Mina what was a good way to make a small bit of money into lots. So we invested the money from the ballet in craft supplies and set up our own business,' said Tilly proudly.

'We're making valentine cards for school,' said Noah, who had quite a lot of sequins stuck to his face. 'I'm doing the decorating.'

'And I am writing beautiful love poems.' Tilly was surrounded by squares of lined paper and pencils. 'What's another word for *kissing*? I'm bored of that, and all I can think of is *lippy cuddles*, and not very much rhymes with that.'

'Ugh, Valentine's Day,' said Sam, looking at a card and screwing up her face.

'Are you not very romantic?' I asked.

She groaned. 'Yuck, no way. But that's not the problem. It's bad enough sharing your birthday with your twin brother. I have to share mine with a million people all whining on about luuuurve and opening their own cards as if I'm not special at all. It's just rude.'

Sam had already handed out her birthday invitations: it was an ice-skating party.

'We'll do you a discount,' said Tilly hopefully. 'Three for two? Buy six, get two more half price? Ten for ten pounds!'

'Tilly!' growled Jem.

'We're only being underpanturinal!' protested Noah.

'Entrepreneurial, you gonk,' said Tilly, slapping him on the head with a gluestick.

Then Spooky leaped onto the table and ran across it, gathering sticky pompoms and glitter as he went – then leaping off to distribute them around the house.

'Er,' I said.

'I'll go,' sighed Jem. 'Have fun with your fairy play whatever.'

She disappeared, and I heard her stomping up the stairs muttering, 'No, Spooky, cats love baths, really they do.'

We left Tilly and Noah to be gluey in the kitchen, and went into the back room.

I laid out the big Hogwarty Shakespeare book on the coffee table, and the Schools Version from Miss Eagle's class.

Someone had turned the giraffe on the mantelpiece round again, so you could see the bump of clear glue sticking the leg on. I turned it back so it looked perfect.

There was still a gap where the ostrich egg used to be. I touched the empty wooden stand where it was meant to fit, feeling sad.

'*In attendance: me, Sam, Georgie*,' said Billie, writing on a clipboard. (She had decided to be Secretary of MEEE, if I was going to be Director.) 'Does Jem really not want to be in MEEE?'

'If she doesn't like acting, she could do hammering like Efe,' suggested Sam. 'Where is Efe, anyway?'

'She had to go to a funeral,' said Billie. 'I think. Something important, anyway.'

'Jem's fine,' I said. 'She knows she can join in if she wants to.'

There was a loud clipping of heeled shoes in the hallway.

'Martin! No! Send Janusz. I want the job done properly. You can get Elise to cover the north-east, and— Oh! Hello, girls. No, not you, Martin, shush.'

Mum walked in, wearing a red trouser suit and a floaty white scarf round her neck, her phone clutched in her hand.

'There it is!' she said, snatching up a folder from the arm of the sofa. 'Sorry, can't stop and chat, there's a car waiting – meeting in Kensington, big yawn.' She paused to flash me a smile. 'So lovely to see you with new friends, darling. Kiss kiss.' She made a smoochy noise with her lips, and whirled away in a cloud of jasmine perfume.

I felt my face go red to the tips of my hair – but the others didn't seem to notice.

'Oh. My. Days,' said Billie, clutching the sofa cushions. 'I thought when you said your mum invented Fairy Dusters you were having me on. But that . . . that was . . . Your mum is *Mina McKay*? The *actual* Mina McKay?'

I nodded.

'Am I supposed to know who that is?' asked Sam.

Billie rolled her eyes. 'She's super famous.'

'She isn't,' I said, squirming. 'Not unless you read *Business Trader Weekly* or saw that one time she was on *This Morning*.'

'My dad totally reads *Business Trader Weekly*! She set up her own business with one little van doing cleaning, and now she's, like, a business superstar. She could be on *Dragon's Den*. She's amazing.' Billie grinned at me. 'You must be dead proud.'

I felt my face go hot again, but for nice reasons. I *was* proud. And she *was* amazing. In lots of ways.

'I'm glad my mums aren't famous,' said Sam, flopping back on the sofa and hugging a cushion. 'If they went on telly I might curl up and die.'

'My mum passed away,' said Billie quietly.

'Sorry,' said Sam. 'I didn't mean it about the curling up and dying.'

'I know. It's OK. I've got my dad still, and he's awesome.'

'Meh,' said Sam. 'Dads. Never really felt the need.'

I could feel Billie looking at me as if she was waiting for me to say something. There was a little crinkle in her forehead, as if she was putting thoughts together in her mind like jigsaw pieces.

'Look at the time! We'd better get on,' I said, thumping the big book open and pulling out my character lists. 'Now, who in our class has the loudest voice?'

And we did MEEE things for the whole of the next two hours, with Billie watching me curiously the whole time.

JEM

Dear Nishat,
  What would make you happy?
  Because curly fries are nice but not that
nice. Have you considered crinkle cut, for
example? Personally I quite like a rustic wedge,
but they are not for everyone.

From Jemima Magee, aged 11¼

It turned out that valentine cards, delivered much
too early, were not what would make Nishat happy.

I bought one off Tilly, who promised to write
her very best love poem inside, and tucked it into
Nishat's locker before we went to tutor group – but
at lunch break we found her weeping in the
changing rooms, clutching a crumply pink card
with neon feathers drooping off it.

'Oh! Did someone give you an early valentine, Nishat?' I said brightly, because sometimes if you ignore the fact that someone's crying, they stop, maybe. 'They must *really* like you.'

'No, they don't!' she sobbed. 'They don't like me at all!'

Georgie took the card and opened it. Her face fell. 'Oh no,' she whispered.

Inside was not Tilly's very best love poem:

Oh! I am stricken with love for my dearest Nishat
I like you even more than our cat
Well actually maybe not that much
But only because our cat is amazing
Ah me! Oh love! KISSES
From ?????

'I think valentines don't count if they're sent early,' I said firmly, shoving the card in my kit bag. 'I expect that one was just someone practising before they sent you the real one.'

Then we had to go and play netball.

That didn't cheer Nishat up, either. Everyone was so keen not to hurt her, no one would throw the ball to her at all. The one time Billie did, she was so busy weeping over her strange valentine that it hit her in the face again, and she had to be taken away to have cotton wool stuffed up her nose.

'It's not my fault!' said Tilly when we got home and shouted at her. 'Hardly anyone's as lovely as Spooky. And poems are really difficult, actually, especially when you have to do lots and lots of them all at once.'

'How many of these have you sold?' asked Georgie, warily picking up another pink card. The poem inside read:

> To Tinkerbell
> You don't smell
> You won't go to hell
> Well
> Hopefully not
> I love you!
> xxx

'No refunds!' snapped Noah, snatching it out of her hand.

As he scurried out clutching an armful of glittery cards, Dad walked in. 'Do I want to know?' he asked warily, yawning. He'd been on early shifts all week, catching little old ladies with maple-cure bacon sandwiches hidden under their hats like upmarket Paddingtons.

'Best not,' I said. 'How would you make someone happy, Dad?'

He frowned. 'Depends who they are, kid. I'd settle for a pair of work shoes that didn't rub, and world peace.'

'Shopping,' said Mina, clicking across the stone floor to the coffee machine. 'Instant cheer. Well, so long as no one tells you what the size is, ha ha!' She laughed tightly. Then she softened, looking at me. 'Oh, Jem, darling, I said I'd take you shopping, didn't I? For nice undies and girly chats. We could do it this weekend – on Saturday morning, before you go off to Bridget's. You too, Georgie, of course, darling.'

Georgie smiled wanly. 'No thanks, Mum. I've got lots of MEEE to get on with.'

'Don't you want to?' I whispered as we went upstairs.

Georgie shuffled her shoulders. 'It's complicated. Um. Sometimes Mum says she'll do a thing – and then work comes up and she does that instead. Don't be cross if that happens, OK?'

It was true. That was how we got to be friends, after all; always being the last ones left in the playground at school. With my mum and dad it was always the other one's fault – they spent about a year refusing to talk to each other, which makes it difficult to arrange who is picking up the children from school. But with Mina it was always work.

'She won't this time, though,' I said firmly. 'Not when she's taking *me*. It'll be fun. And, like, an important bonding moment. After that she'll definitely like me.' I hated shopping, but I did want some bras like that blue one. And, just maybe, after we'd done the bonding, she'd give me that necklace with the amethysts on it, I thought – though I didn't say that to Georgie.

'She likes you already, silly,' she said. 'Ooh! I know how to help Nishat! She could be in MEEE! We don't really have enough people to do any of the play yet. She could do a dance, or read some lines, or paint some scenery . . . There's got to be something she'd like . . .'

To be honest, usually I would just do a happiness spell where you eat some cheese on toast. (You have to stand on one leg while you're doing it or it's not a spell. I'm not telling you which leg, though.) But Georgie is better at some things than I am, like guessing people's feelings.

Georgie wrote her a special invitation with gel-pen flowers on the envelope.

Dear Nishat,
 You are cordially invited to our house after school on Thursday, for dinner. We are doing a play for Miss Eagle, for when she comes back, and we think you'd be very good in it. Please come.

From Georgie and Jem

Nishat looked petrified when she read it. 'Is it like an audition?' she whispered.

'Yes,' said Georgie.

'I don't want to,' said Nishat.

'Then no,' said Georgie. 'It won't be anything like an audition.'

Nishat nodded reluctantly.

On Thursday after school we walked home together: Nishat, me and Georgie, Sam on her bike, and Billie.

The back room had been set up exactly as it had been for the ballet, ready for a performance, with the sofa pulled round to be the audience. Tilly, Noah and Spooky were already there, waiting to watch.

'Now,' said Georgie. 'Have you ever been in a play? Sung a song? Danced a dance? Are you familiar with the language of the sixteenth century? Are you more of a duke, or a fairy, or a man with a donkey head on?'

It was nice, seeing Georgie being all in charge.

But Nishat said no to everything.

Georgie tried teaching her a series of steps, but she tripped over her own feet.

Georgie asked her to be a fairy, but she just lay on the floor, very stiff.

'I'm a fairy that's asleep,' she squeaked.

Tilly and Noah clapped.

'You are very good at that,' Georgie said slowly. 'Perhaps . . .'

She made Nishat stand up, led her to the middle of the stage and lifted her arms up and out.

'This whole play happens in a forest. Could you be a tree?'

Nishat stood perfectly rigid, with her eyes shut and her arms sticking out.

Tilly and Noah clapped so hard that Spooky leaped into the air and hid under the sofa.

'Is it any good?' Nishat asked, cracking open one eye.

'It's magical,' said Georgie, beaming. 'Well done. You should be very proud of yourself.'

Nishat beamed too.

For dinner we had quiche and salad.

'I asked if we could have curly fries,' Georgie hissed out of the side of her mouth.

'And I ignored you, sweetheart, because we have guests and we feed guests proper food,' said Dad, passing Nishat a bowl of warm potatoes. 'Help yourself, lovely.'

Nishat nibbled at her quiche like a little rabbit. But when her dad came to pick her up, she gave both me and Georgie a tight hug. 'Thank you! I'm very happy about being a tree!'

I was happy too.

'USS is going to work,' Georgie whispered, ticking Nishat off her list of names in the back of her English book. 'It's really going to work.'

Until Friday morning's Geography lesson, which was all about insect migration.

'Bzzz,' said Big Mohammad.

'Arrrrgh!' yelped Nishat, and leaped under her desk. 'Is it gone? Is it still there? I will stay here until there are definitely no bees!'

Halid threw a pencil at Big Mohammad's head.

We all promised Nishat there were no bees, but she spent the rest of Geography being passed rubbers and rulers, drawing a population pyramid from her safe space on the floor.

'But if Nishat is afraid of bees . . .' said Georgie, whispering in my ear.

'Then the curly-fries secret wasn't hers at all.'

'Oh well, never mind. Being in the play will make her happy anyway,' said Georgie, hardly sounding disappointed at all. She opened up her MEEE folder under her Geography textbook to a page marked *Director's Notes*, and wrote, *Memo to Efe for set design: remember, no bees on stage!*

GEORGIE

'If it's not Nishat who only feels happy with curly fries, then it *has* to be Alfie; he's the only other one who had seconds,' I said, staring at the USS list that evening. 'Maybe we should invite him round for auditions and dinner too.'

Jem scrunched up her face. 'He's annoying, though. He puts out his tongue and makes sexy noises outside the netball courts. I don't want him being pervy at our house. What if Tilly falls in love with him?'

'I don't want him being pervy in my play, either. I mean, Miss Eagle's play. Even if he is only pervy because he's unhappy.'

Jem lay on my bed and stared at the USS list thoughtfully.

Lunch-box thief
~~Curly fries~~ ALFIE

Secret chess wizard
Never kissed anyone
Goldfish murderer
~~Scared of bees~~ NISHAT

'I wonder who the secret chess wizard is. Like, why would you not want to tell everyone how good you are at a thing?'

I sighed, giving her a gentle pat on the head. Jem is brilliant at a lot of things, but not at understanding what it is like to be shy, or the sort of clever that even teachers find annoying. The secret chess wizard was bound to be shy and clever.

'I think I might take up a new hobby,' I said at lunch time the next day, very casually. 'Like . . . oh, I don't know. Chess? If only there was someone in our class who could help me learn . . .'

Jem kicked me under the table *and* glared, even though I was doing excellent subtle research.

'I know no things about chess,' said Efe. 'Apart from what was in one book that I read one time. That is all I know about chess.' She shuffled awkwardly in her seat.

'Are you all right?' asked Sam.

Efe chewed a fingernail.

'She went to a funeral, remember?' hissed Billie. 'Are you very sad still?'

'Yes,' said Efe solemnly. 'All of the sadness.'

Billie gave her half her twirly pastry. Then she discovered that her apple had a big bite out of it, so I gave her half my biscuit, and it was rather difficult to go back to talking about chess.

It turned out not to matter. On our way across the playground at the end of break, Jem gripped my wrist tightly.

'Look!' she hissed.

Madison and Lianne were walking right ahead of us, Madison's school bag bouncing against her hip above her very short skirt: a plasticky satchel with a pattern of purple and black chess pieces.

'No,' I whispered back. 'Not Madison. It couldn't be.'

She wasn't shy or clever. She was the sort of person who put up lists calling people fat and giving them marks out of ten, after all. She spent most of every lesson pinging pencils at Lianne. She was much more interested in boys than in serious strategy games; you could tell that just by looking.

But now that I was actually looking, she did seem to be paying very close attention to Mr Cole in Geography. And she only started pinging pencils across the Maths room after twenty minutes because she'd already finished all the questions – and even I still had nine left.

Could Madison be a secret genius underneath all her orangey make-up?

'There's only one way to find out,' said Jem, grabbing my arm and marching me up to Madison at the end of the day. 'Hi! My sister wanted to ask you something.'

Madison turned, arching one well-plucked eyebrow when she saw who it was. Lianne narrowed her eyes, all ferrety. I felt very small and ordinary all of a sudden, with my long pleated skirt and my face that was just a face.

But then Madison's eyes lit up. 'Ooh! Nishat says you're doing a play thing for Miss Eagle. I want to do that. I can't do acting, though –'cos, duh.' She pointed at her mouth. She had two rows of braces, which I'd never really noticed before. I had no idea why they meant she couldn't do acting; lots of the Dance Magic girls had them.

'You should do make-up,' said Lianne, nudging her. 'Madison's, like, the best at make-up.'

'Yes!' said Jem. 'Make-up! Georgie should come to your house and you can practise on her face.'

'I should?' I mumbled.

And suddenly Madison was typing her address into my phone. 'Saturday morning. Before twelve, 'cos I've got swimming.'

'Brilliant,' said Jem as we joined the others to walk home.

'Is it, though?' I whispered.

'Of course. Think of all the volcanoes we're putting out.'

When we were eating breakfast on Saturday morning, Mum was already in her office, having a panic about furniture polish with a distraught lorry driver from Birmingham.

'She says she'll be finished soon,' said Jem cheerfully, eating porridge with honey. 'And then she has to make one more phone call, and *then* we'll go shopping.'

I smiled tightly.

'Sure she will, kiddo,' said Joel, squeezing her shoulder when he saw my face. 'Now, Georgie – I hear you need a lift?'

We edged past the littles in the hallway on the way out to the car.

'We haven't borrowed anything,' said Tilly loudly, through her hair.

'We have borrowed no things at all,' said Noah, nodding.

They were both sitting on something long and narrow, wrapped in three jumpers.

'Glad to hear it,' I said.

Joel drove me all the way to Willesden, anxiously tapping his hands on the steering wheel.

'Your ma *will* take Jem out, won't she?' he asked.

'Um. Maybe? She'll definitely mean to.'

He grinned. 'I'll give her a nudge if she looks like forgetting. Here we go – number 123? Well now. And I thought our place was roomy.'

Madison's house turned out to be enormous, with a huge driveway lined with square-cut bushes, and white pillars outside the glossy wood front door. And the girl who came to the door was almost unrecognizable. She was wearing a neat white blouse covered in little blue flowers, baggy grey jeans, her hair was swept back with a pink alice band, and she wasn't orange-faced at all.

Then she grinned and shouted, 'Oh my days!' in my ear, and suddenly she was Madison again.

'You came! I can't believe you came. Lianne said, *She'll never come*, and I said, *Yeah, she will*, and Lianne said, *Nah*, and I said, *Yuh-huh*, and Lianne said, *No, but really*, and I said, *Yeah, but really* – and now you're here. That's really nice of you. I really want to do the play thing. I love plays. I've seen *A Midsummer Night's Dream*, like, ten times, probably? Only I never said, 'cos, duh, you can't go round telling people you like plays. Well, *you* can. But me? Nah. You know what I mean?'

I nodded. I *did* know.

And I knew that someone who liked plays and didn't want anyone to know was bound to be a secret chess wizard.

She pulled me up a long wide staircase with a deep blue carpet, and into a huge bedroom with pink flowered wallpaper and frilly white bedlinen. The room was lined with three bookshelves, crammed full of books – with crinkled spines, so you knew they had been read. There were lots I had on my shelves too: *Harry Potter* and Jacqueline Wilson; *Malory Towers* and *Murder Most Unladylike*. There was a desk, very neat, with all the pencils in pots and homework in neat piles.

I liked it almost as much as my own bedroom, except it wasn't lavender.

Madison pulled open a large wardrobe and tugged out a plain white shirt. 'Why don't you put this on? Then I won't get any make-up on your top.'

She stood waiting with her back to me, hands on hips, while I wriggled out of my cardigan and long-sleeved top.

The shirt was a bit small, and very tight round the arms. I didn't mind. I have a dancer's body, which means I'm lean and long, and people are often surprised at my clothes size because I look slim but I have muscles, and my shoulders are broad.

I leaned forward and looked at my reflection in the mirror over the dressing table, checking I'd lined the buttons up right.

Then I saw something else in the mirror.

A small wire cage perched on top of the chest of drawers beside the bed, filled with sawdust and wood shavings, with a wheel and a water bottle attached.

A hamster.

My heart did a flip.

'Ready? Good. I've got loads of ideas . . .'

Madison sat me down on the stool with a firm press on my shoulders, and stood behind me, beaming at our reflections. She pulled out various pointy-looking pencils and blood-red lipsticks from a glass bowl sitting by the mirror.

A big, curving, almost perfectly spherical glass bowl.

Like a goldfish bowl.

With no goldfish in it.

Madison picked up a pair of eyelash curlers, like scissors gone wrong, snapping them delightedly.

'Where shall we start?' she said.

JEM

Dear Mina,

    I have been quite looking forward to you taking me out for shopping and girly chats, actually.

    I don't mind if we don't even do the shopping part. We could just talk and watch telly. I'm quite interesting, actually. I know you mostly ask me about homework and if I've done it, and laundry and why my socks are on the floor not in the basket, and how biscuits ended up in the shopping trolley again, but those aren't really my favourite things.

    It doesn't have to be this morning even.

    Just whenever.

    If you can fit it in.

From Jemima Magee, aged 11¼

'Just one more call,' mouthed Mina for the third time.

I sat on the floor outside her office for a bit, rearranging the vases.

Then I went upstairs and looked through my craft box, which is full of old, worn-out shirts and fabric from the charity shop, and wool that's gone wiggly because I've already made something with it and unravelled it when I got bored. But all the projects I wanted to do would take ages, and then I'd have to leave to try on bras for 'girl time', and it didn't seem worth it.

I went downstairs again, and rearranged the giraffe on the shelf so it was facing the right way and you could see its bumpy leg.

I packed our bags for going to Croydon.

I even put things in the dishwasher.

The clock ticked round to ten o'clock. Mum would be coming sometime after twelve. I didn't think it would take me very long to buy bras – I only wanted blue ones – but I thought girly chats might take longer.

I was just about to tap on Mina's door again when the doorbell rang.

When I opened it, I found a small black man in a suit, with lots of curly hair and silver glasses. He was carrying a small case and looking nervous.

'We don't want to buy any,' I said, because he was probably selling something and I needed all my money for bras.

'Oh!' he said. 'Sorry. Should've introduced. Didn't think. Silly me. Martin.' He stuck out a hand, smiling sheepishly.

I shook it.

There was a weird pause when he seemed to think I'd know what to do next.

'Sorry. Didn't think again. Martin. From the office. Mina. Need to see. Hmm?'

I let him in then: Mina was always talking about Martin – usually not very nicely because of something he'd forgotten – and I thought someone ought to be nice to him.

'Martin! Thank God. Come in!' said Mina when I tapped on the door. He disappeared inside with a squeak as she carried on talking into the phone.

I made him a cup of coffee because it seemed officey, and also so I could go into the office to remind Mina that we were going out to buy bras and have girl time, right now.

But before I could knock Martin reappeared in the hallway, looking very flustered and stuttery.

'Er. Jemima?' he said, adjusting his glasses.

'That's me. Everyone calls me Jem.'

'Jem. Very good. Well. Shall we? This way? Car. Outside.'

I followed him out, pulling on my coat. 'Is Mina coming in a minute?'

Martin pulled a face. 'Very busy. Big problem. Lorry crash. Furniture polish everywhere. So. Just us. And . . . credit card?'

He produced a shiny gold card from his coat pocket, and looked even more flustered.

To be honest, I didn't really want to go and buy bras and have girl chats with Martin, especially since he didn't seem very good at sentences. I quite wanted to go back inside and say, *Georgie warned me about this, and I said you were too nice to not take me shopping*, until Mina felt horribly guilty. But I thought Martin would probably get into trouble, and a small corner of me wondered if maybe she wasn't coming because she didn't like me after all. So instead I got in the car and we went to Westfield.

We went to one bra shop after another, but nowhere had blue ones like the one I'd seen before. Martin kept taking off his glasses and wiping them on his tie so he didn't have to look at any knickers. Eventually I gave up and took him to Starbucks for a calming peppermint tea; while he paid, I whispered comforting words over it to make it a bit magic.

'How do you feel about the Fairy Dusters logo, Martin?' I asked him, eating my gingerbread biscuit.

'Well. Gosh. Er. Distinctive. Strong brand reach. Well-established. Humorous, yet associated with quality. Hmm. Yes.'

'But, Martin,' I said, 'have you considered the reality of actual fairies? Like, in history?'

And I told him all about them not being wandy with tutus, and in fact prone to sneakily pretending to be logs, stealing innocent babies, and generally being a pain in the bum.

'Hmm. Yes. I see. Something to be. Hmm. Next board meeting. Marketing. Have a word.

Very kind.' He nudged his glasses again. 'Heavens. Almost twelve. In trouble.' He gave a little giggle.

Then he drove us excitingly fast back to Kensal Rise, and screeched up the drive with a big whoosh of gravel.

Mum's car drove up right behind us.

'Oh. Hi. Hmm. Martin. Very nice. Meet you,' he said, shaking Mum's hand rather warily.

She was wearing her big clumpy boots, stripy green tights, lightning-bolt earrings and a floaty dress with shiny peacock-feather eyes embroidered all over it. I felt quite relieved I didn't have a posh blue bra after all; suddenly it seemed much more of a smart, businessy Mina sort of a thing than a quirky, witchy Mum one.

'Is that young man all right?' she asked, giving me a hug as he hurried inside.

'He will be now I've told him all about fairies.'

Mum grinned. 'No wonder he looked so worried. Now, where are my two small horrors, eh? Tills! Nono!'

'Lloyd Park! Frisbee golf!' I yelled into the back room – but it was empty.

The front one was empty too – and the bedrooms upstairs, except for Dad, asleep after his late shift. I checked the bathrooms and the garden, but there was no one there except Spooky. The bags were packed by the door where I'd left them. Mina was in her office, shouting something at Martin about an unacceptable lack of lemony freshness. But Tilly and Noah were nowhere at all. The pegs where their coats and hats lived were empty.

'They're gone!' I yelped, feeling all worried and big sisterish.

'What d'you mean, *gone*?'

'Gone!' I shouted, stamping my foot.

At that Mina came out. 'I am on a business call, you know,' she started to say, very crossly. Then she saw Bridget, and her face shifted. 'I'll call you back in ten,' she said, tucking the phone away.

'Where would they go, Jem?' said Mum, ignoring her and leaning down so her face was right in mine. 'Would they run off? Have they run away?'

'Run away?' said Mina. 'What? You don't think— Tilly? Noah!'

She came back after a few minutes, looking pale. 'They're gone,' she whispered.

'Can I? Helpful?' mumbled Martin.

'No!' said both Mum and Mina together.

'I'm calling the police,' said Mina.

'I think they might have gone shopping, maybe,' I said slowly. 'Why don't we split up and search first? I'll look there, you check with the neighbours to see if they know anything . . .'

'I'll wring their wee necks . . . once I've hugged them to death . . . Oh, on my visitation day – *whyyy* . . .'

Outside, Mum turned right. Mina and Martin crossed the road and knocked on the Paget-Skidelskys' door. I went left, and walked double quick up Sorrel Street, over the railway bridge, as far as The Splendide – but I could hear them long before that.

Tilly was playing Georgie's violin.

Noah was singing while banging on the violin-case lid like a drum.

My felt hat with the purple flower sewn on it was on the ground in front of them, filled with a scattering of copper coins and a few silver ones.

Help the Homeless said a cardboard sign beside it, written in green felt pen. There was a small crowd too, blocking the pavement and filled with people looking sort of terrified.

'Shut up! Stop! You two are in all sorts of trouble!' I yelled, running up to them and grabbing Tilly's arm mid-bow.

We Wish You a Merry Christmas stopped abruptly.

Noah pouted, pointing at the hat. 'We're doing really well, though.'

'You're lying!' I said, snatching up the sign. 'You're not homeless!'

'We never said we were,' said Tilly crossly, snatching up the hat as the crowd began to murmur and grumble. 'We just put out a sign that says people should help the homeless. Because they should. And then we just happened to stand next to it. By coincidence.'

'We were being underpanturinal again,' said Noah.

'You were being massive fibbers,' I told them sternly. 'And running away and making everyone panic. Now come home before you get arrested.'

Tilly stuck out her tongue (the little pink tip just about reached through her hair) – but at just that moment a police officer happened to walk past on the other side of the road. With a squeak, Tilly thrust the violin into its case, and the three of us hurried away, Noah turning back to wave farewell to his audience.

Then we ran all the way down Sorrel Street.

Mum couldn't decide whether to hug them or shout at them – so she did both at the same time.

'Oh!' said Mina. 'You two . . . And you, Jem – I didn't . . . And the lorries . . . Oh!' And she burst into tears in the middle of the road.

I'd seen Mum cry loads, because of all the stupid man-friends. But seeing Mina go from all perfectly lipsticked and crisp-suited to a ball of snot felt very odd; like looking at her internal organs, even though I knew she liked to keep those private.

'Oh, sweetheart – there, there, no harm done,' said Mum, wrapping her arms round Mina and guiding her back into the house. 'No broken bones, no lost dogs . . .'

'Nothing that can't be fixed,' we all chorused together.

'Put the kettle on, Jem, eh? Martin, why don't you finish that phone call for Mina? And – where will I find the biscuits?'

Ten minutes later Mum and Mina were chatting away in the kitchen, Mum telling Mina about all the times Noah had got lost in the cheese aisle in Tesco.

I sat on the stairs with Tilly and Noah, being very stern and big-sisterly about donating all the money they'd made to a proper homeless charity.

'But we need it,' protested Tilly.

'Or we won't be able to buy . . .' mumbled Noah.

They both made the shape of an egg with their hands.

'You know – you could just tell Mina that it was you two who broke it,' I said, tucking a rope of hair behind one of Tilly's ears so I could see one green eye. 'She's used to us now. She'll be cross, but she won't kick us out.'

Tilly shook her head, glaring fiercely. 'No. We're going to fix it. Fixing things is what we do.'

The front door banged open and closed.

Georgie appeared, her face covered in alarming bright colours, her arms wrapped round her, and a strange wriggly something happening inside her cardigan.

'Hello! I'm just— I'll be— Help!'

'What happened to your face?' asked Tilly.

'Make-up.'

'What's happening in your jumper?' asked Noah.

Then Georgie let out a little scream, and a tiny brown face appeared at the top of her collar, just under her chin.

'Is everything all right?' called Mina.

'Yes!' I said very loudly as the brown thing disappeared back inside the cardigan and began to wriggle down Georgie's sleeve.

'Madison isn't a secret chess wizard! She's a secret goldfish murderer!'

'So you stole her hamster?' asked Tilly.

'Yes! Obviously!' Georgie looked furious. 'And – it bit me! A lot! All the way home!'

She pulled up her sleeve to show off the bite marks – and the hamster shot out, rolled across the floor and then scuttled off to hide behind a vase.

Spooky padded down the stairs, yawning.

'Oh no,' I whispered. 'Quick!'

Tilly made a grab for Spooky – and missed.

I lifted up the vase – but the hamster shot out from behind it and scurried off into the back room and under the sofa, pursued by a cat.

We all chased after it.

'Here!' yelped Noah as the hamster zigzagged desperately across the floor and under the other sofa.

Spooky prowled, sniffing, darting out one paw.

The hamster shot out from behind the sofa and quivered in a corner.

'Now!' I yelled.

Tilly jumped forward and wrapped it in her hands – but it bit her too, and escaped once again, running back into the hall.

I grabbed a blue vase with elephants on, up-ended it, chased the hamster into another corner – and finally managed to trap it underneath.

'We should do this again,' Mina was saying in a sniffly voice as she and Mum came out of the kitchen.

'Preferably without quite so much panic, eh?'

They hugged.

'Come on then, you horrible lot. Into the car with you. And don't go thinking I've finished telling you off yet. We're going to have a long talk about why children don't go off by themselves without telling anyone . . . or borrow other people's violins without asking . . . or take up busking . . . and all the lovely ways you're going to make it up to Mina for worrying her so much . . .'

Behind them, the upturned vase began slowly walking itself across the hall.

'What's that noise?' asked Mina.

'Nothing!' I said loudly, beginning to hum a tune. 'Let's go! Bye!'

I left Georgie to fix it. I think being good with vases probably runs in her family.

GEORGIE

'I'm sorry about Mum,' I told Jem on Sunday night, once she'd come back from Croydon. 'She doesn't mean to crush your hopes and dreams. It just happens.'

Jem sighed philosophically. 'I know. Mine's the same. But if our parents weren't hopeless, then we'd never have met in the playground, and then we wouldn't be sisters. So it's for the best really.'

I liked that Jem always found a way to be cheerful.

Even about the hamster, which had turned out to be so horrible I could completely see why Madison had murderous feelings. We'd found it a home in Tilly's shoebox doll's house. It slept all day, and stayed up all night making nibbling noises. Its favourite thing to eat was fingers. And it did a row of small brown poos in my left slipper. But Jem declared she had a cunning plan, and on

Monday took it to school in a cake tin with holes punched in the lid, filled with tasty crumbs. She left it outside Alfie's locker, with a glitter- and poem-free card from Tilly and Noah's stash.

Dear Alfie,
    Here is a hamster. We think it is a girl but we aren't sure so we are calling it 'they'. I don't know what their real name is. We suggest:

    Bitey McBiterson
    Cloris Morris
    A swear (the person who thought this had just had their slipper pooped in, so please be understanding)
    Popcorn

    I hope they make you happy!

Madison didn't say a word about her hamster – or the fact that Alfie had one in a cake tin in his locker.

'See?' Jem said, proudly watching as Alfie spent all his lunch hour feeding it carrot sticks. 'We've completely saved its life *and* made Alfie happy.'

'Will it definitely make him happy?' I asked doubtfully as we walked towards the picnic benches.

'Yes,' she said. 'That's what pets do.'

'What are you whispering about?' asked Billie, popping up behind us.

'Nothing!' said Jem, in the sort of voice that made it sound a lot like something.

'Nothing important,' I mumbled.

I quite wanted to tell Billie all about USS. Especially my thrilling hamster rescue. But it was nice having something that was just for me and Jem too.

'The lunch-box thief strikes again,' said Sam sadly, opening her lunch box as we all sat down.

She was missing a packet of almonds, and Billie's cheese-and-onion pasty had been cut in half.

'It's as if they wanted you to still have *some* lunch,' I said slowly. 'Like they didn't want to be completely mean.'

234

'Oh, how generous,' said Sam, rolling her eyes. 'Argh! I've had enough. I want to catch them. We'll put video cameras over the lunch boxes. Or *in* the lunch boxes. Or in my bag of almonds.'

'When the salon next door to us got broken into, they'd put special sticky blue paint all over the back gate,' said Billie, looking thoughtful. 'So the burglars had sticky blue paint on them. It doesn't even come off in the wash. I know, because I poked it with my elbow and now my red hoodie is totally messed up for ever.'

'I don't want paint in my lunch,' said Efe.

'Food colouring!' said Sam. 'Mum K's been practising rainbow birthday cakes – there's loads at my house. It gets everywhere. I'm going to squirt a big blob in all my sandwiches and down the middle of my banana – and then whoever is pinching them will have a bright blue tongue. Then we'll catch them red-handed. Well, sort of.'

'We'll all do it. Right?' said Billie.

'Right,' said Jem, so I nodded too.

'It's like they're working for USS on the side,' she said, back at home. 'Without knowing. And with us not telling them they are. It's fine.'

'But . . . I don't want to catch the lunch-box thief exactly,' I said quietly. 'Aren't we meant to be helping them turn their volcano into an ordinary internal mountain?'

Mum wasn't convinced either.

'We're doing an experiment,' Jem explained. 'So for lunch tomorrow I can't have salad any more. I have to have sandwiches. Or cake. Or sausage rolls. Anything you can hide something inside.'

Mum sighed, tilting her head on one side, and patted Jem's hand. 'Oh, darling. I was just like you at your age, you know.'

I had no idea she was the sort of person who put blue food colouring in sausage rolls to catch lunch-box thieves. But then she stroked a hand over her tummy, where it stuck out a bit over her work trousers, and sighed tragically.

'I have to work so hard to stay slim. I don't want that for you, Jem.'

'Neither do I,' said Jem. 'So let's not bother.'

Mum sat down hard, and stared at Jem as if she had just invented electricity or started speaking fluent Spanish. She didn't say anything, all through dinner.

But the next day Jem's lunch box had a sandwich in it. A salady one, on brown bread with bits in, but still a sandwich.

Sam handed out little tubes of colouring to each of us at the gates, first thing. Jem lifted the top layer of bread, squirted a good thick layer of blue all over the tomatoes, and put it back. Billie chose green. Sam went for a dramatic red. Efe chose orange.

'No, thank you,' I said. 'I prefer my lunch to be unadulterated by chemicals.'

I was very relieved when we got to lunch time. Half my sandwich was gone – along with a triangle of cheese, a bag of carrot sticks, two apples, and all Billie's cheesy pastry plait. But when we prowled around Mr Miller's classroom before afternoon lessons, hunting for telltale tongues and stained teeth, the only ones were Jem's, Sam's, Billie's and Efe's.

'We didn't think this through,' said Billie, inspecting her alarmingly green mouth in the screen of her phone.

'I don't know – I kind of like it,' said Sam, sticking out her scary red tongue. 'It did taste a bit gluey, though. And, I mean, it probably isn't poisonous. But if any of you die, I'm really sorry.'

'No! It wasn't all a bad idea, don't you see?' I said. 'If no one's got green teeth and blue tongues – apart from you – then whoever's taking the food isn't eating it. They're taking it *somewhere else*.'

'So?' said Jem.

'So . . .' I trailed off. I didn't know. It just seemed important, somehow.

The next day no one put food colouring in their lunches at all – but this time, instead of taking Sam's hummus wrap or bag of almonds, something was left behind. A small square of paper with a line of emojis printed off a computer.

'Oh my days,' said Billie. 'Is the lunch-box thief calling us pigs? That's bang out of order.'

'Maybe it means they will murder us if we don't give them our lunch,' said Efe.

'I think it means . . .' said Sam slowly. 'I have no idea.'

I couldn't work it out either.

The next day there was another small square of paper, printed again.

> IT MEANT PLEASE DON'T PUT FOOD COLOURING IN THE FOOD.
> I'M AWFULLY SORRY. IT WON'T BE FOR EVER.

'Are we getting letters from a pig now?' asked Jem.

'It's a very polite pig,' said Sam.

'It's well cheeky,' said Billie. 'Like they know exactly what they're doing, and they just don't care.'

'I expect they care a lot,' I said quietly. Then I realized that everyone was looking at me curiously. 'It's not me! I promise!'

They all promised.

But none of us had any more idea who the thief was, apart from being someone clever enough not to show us their handwriting.

*

'Don't worry,' said Sam the next day. 'I have had a brilliant idea. That's what happens when you're about to be twelve. They just explode out of you. We're going to catch them at my ice-skating birthday party. Using *mousetraps*.'

'I don't think I can come to this birthday party,' said Efe very quickly. 'I have a prior engagement. At another ice-skating birthday party. It is a strange coincidence.'

'I don't think anyone will, if you put mousetraps in the sandwiches,' said Billie.

'Not in *all* the sandwiches. Just a special selection. And we'll know not to eat those ones.'

'She won't really, will she?' I asked on the way home.

'She might,' said Jem.

JEM

Dear lunch-box thief,
   Georgie says she doesn't want to catch you really but I totally do. You owe me a lot of crisps.

From Jemima Magee, aged 11¼

The twins' ice-skating birthday party was at Alexandra Palace. It was a huge posh building with lots of arches and domes and fancy windows, and trees and gardens and a long drive.

'Is this definitely the right place, lads?' asked Dad, walking us up the path.

'Definitely,' said Georgie. 'Look.'

Sam and the other Sam were waving frantically at us from a queue of people outside, both holding helium balloons and wearing pointy party hats.

Their two mums were wearing hats as well. Dr Paget looked very giggly and excited. Dr Skidelsky looked as if someone had threatened her with large weapons to make her wear hers, and she hadn't forgiven them yet.

'Have fun, lads,' said Dad, hurrying away to buy some extra roses. (He'd given Mina one, wrapped in cellophane. Mina had given him three rose trees, which she'd had planted in the back garden with big purple bows on.)

'I found out I'm in the Kensal Rise Kestrels!' Sam yelled, jumping up and down as we got closer.

'Happy birthday!' I said, jumping too.

We both gave her presents. I'd knitted her a dog badge. Georgie gave her a diary. We gave the other Sam some chocolate.

They both shouted, 'Thanks!' and stuffed everything in Dr Skidelsky's pockets.

Sam pulled us aside.

'The shop wouldn't let me buy twenty-six mousetraps,' she said crossly. 'Though I did try to use Mum Gen's credit card, so it might have been that. And anyway, they do their own catering here, so I couldn't put blue stuff in the sandwiches. And' – she looked around furtively – 'I got periods. Or, well, one. It started last night at midnight. Like it knew it was my birthday. Don't ever be twelve. It is the *worst*.'

'I did say no refunds,' I said, thinking guiltily of jam.

'It's OK. I made the team already. My mums are being super-nice to me. And I still haven't got boobies, so it could be worse. Though I am a tiny bit in massive trouble for inviting the whole class and sort of not telling anyone.'

Dr Skidelsky was gritting her teeth as Halid and Alfie and Big Mohammad did the sort of play-fighting that makes other mums look round and tut.

Dr Paget hurried over. 'So, I have good news and bad news. Because we're a . . . er, slightly larger group than expected, they can't let us on the ice right away – there are lessons going on behind a rope, and we'll need the whole rink. But they will let us come in and watch, and we can have our party lunch *before* we skate, instead of afterwards!'

'It's a quarter to ten,' said Dr Skidelsky. 'There is not a child on this planet who would want fish fingers and chips at this hour.'

'Oh, I expect it'll take a little while to come. And they'll keep some warm for us. And it'll give us time to get our skates on before we go on the ice. Also – perhaps today might go a little more smoothly if you tried not having an awful time, Kara, dear, don't you think?' Dr Paget's smile went thin round the edges.

'We can totally eat chips at a quarter to ten, miss,' said Halid.

'That's nice, dear, thank you,' said Dr Paget.

'Next year we are taking two friends to the cinema like normal people,' said Dr Skidelsky, folding her arms.

It was freezing cold inside the palace place. We all took off our shoes and swapped them for pairs of heavy blue ice skates that smelled a bit. Then we went upstairs to a café overlooking the ice rink through big arched windows. There were drinks and cups laid out on long tables, and two sweaty boys in waistcoats were bringing platters heaped with hot fish fingers and mini pizzas. We put on our skates, and awkwardly moonwalked across to lean over the rails and watch the skaters having a lesson out on the ice.

There were three: one boy wearing a sparkly top doing a lot of spins, one tiny little girl who was doing jumps, and one grown-up woman with short curly blonde hair, who looked a bit lumpy round her middle.

'I'm going to do that,' said Alfie as the tiny girl leaped into the air.

'I'm going to do that,' said the boy Sam as the sparkly-top boy stopped sharply in a shower of icy flakes.

'I'm probably going to be her,' I sighed as the grown-up woman tried to skate backwards and fell on her face.

'She got straight back up again, though,' said Georgie kindly.

Then the grown-up woman's feet slid out from under her, and this time she fell on her bottom.

'Oh,' said Georgie.

But the woman got back up again, and kept skating backwards without falling for quite a while. She had nice leggings on: purple, with silver stars.

'You know,' said Georgie, 'it's funny, but don't you think she looks a bit like . . .'

The grown-up woman sped up, skating past the sparkly-top boy and suddenly switching to skating forward without even stopping. She raised a hand in the air in triumph – then her skate seemed to catch on something lumpy on the ice, and she tumbled over once again, sliding flat on her tummy into the wall. She lay breathing hard, raising one arm in a thumbs-up to signal she wasn't hurt. Then she rolled over and hooted with laughter, the sound ringing around the ice rink like a bell.

'Isn't that—?' Georgie whispered.

'Mum?!' I yelled.

I ran as fast as I could down the stairs – which was not very, in ice skates.

By the time I got down to the same level as the rink she was up on her feet again, gliding backwards.

'Mum!' I yelled again, dashing through the door that led onto the rink. 'Muuuuum!'

I jumped onto the ice.

It was slippy. Very, very, very slippy. My feet skidded out from underneath me at once, and I sat down hard, *thump*, on the ice.

'Ow!'

At last she saw me.

Her mouth dropped open and she clapped her hands over her face. Then she skated at speed right over to me, skidding to a sharp halt and showering fluffy icy snowflakes over my woolly tights.

'Jem! My love! What—? Why are you—?'

'Never mind that! You can ice-skate! You can, like, really properly ice-skate! Well, kind of.'

Mum giggled. 'Kind of, yes! I've been having lessons. That's what I've been busy with lately, sweetheart – why I had to rush off sometimes on our weekends. I wanted to do something just for me. Only I didn't want you to find out until I was a bit better at it really.' Her cheeks went red. 'I do still fall over a lot.'

It was so exciting I didn't even mind having a wet bottom. I gave her a big hug. Then I told her how I'd thought she had a man-friend, and how I'd been a bit cross about it actually, and how being a secret ice-skater was loads better, even one who fell over a lot.

I gave her another hug, and then I made her come upstairs so she could tell Georgie all about it too.

As we got there, the Sams' mums came in with two cakes lit up with candles, and everyone started singing *Happy Birthday*. Sam's cake had black-and-white icing like a football. Her brother's had red icing and the word *KAPOW!* written on like in a superhero comic.

We all cheered as they blew out their candles.

'I bet I won't be able to skate as well as your mum,' Sam whispered in my ear.

I felt glowy and warm, even though it was freezing and I still had a wet bum.

'Right! Onto the ice, everyone!' announced Dr Skidelsky. 'And try not to vomit fizzy orange everywhere, even though you only ate five minutes ago and this is a terrible idea!'

Everyone went carefully downstairs – except for Edmond Hudson, who wasn't allowed to ice-skate, just to watch.

It was just as slippy this time. I clung onto the side very tightly, and sort of shuffled round and round.

Meanwhile Halid was whizzing around the rink in a pair of heavy hockey boots he'd brought with him, darting up to a wobbly Big Mohammad and Alfie, and stopping very suddenly so they fell over in surprise, then whizzing away cackling.

Most people were somewhere in between. Sam got very excited about being able to go all the way round without holding onto the sides. Billie tried skating backwards, though apparently it was much harder than it had looked when Mum did it, so she kept falling over too. Georgie was quite nervous, but once she got going she was really good, because of dancers having natural grace and balance and also a polar-bear hat.

After a bit I got tired of going round and round, and I might have been crying ever so slightly about how actually ice skating was really difficult, and wet, and not fun at all, so I just watched. Mum was helping Billie with backwardsness. Sam was chasing her brother and cackling. I couldn't see Georgie anywhere – until I turned and saw her heading back up the stairs to the café.

From where I stood I could see the two long picnic tables, still covered with party tablecloths and balloons and leftover food . . . and also, between them, a curly blond head, moving carefully and secretly, emptying carrot sticks and cold mini pizzas into a brown satchel.

'Edmond Hudson is the lunch-box thief!' I yelled, throwing out a pointy finger.

Nobody heard me, because ice rinks are very loud, so I waited till Sam skated past me again, then waved her and Billie over. We all sneaked back upstairs, where Georgie was hovering anxiously by the picnic tables, whispering with a very worried-looking Edmond Hudson. He was hugging his satchel tightly.

'You! Lunch-box thief!' said Sam.

Edmond lowered his head guiltily.

Georgie took a step forward. 'It's not what you think! Don't shout at him – it's not his fault.'

'The food just jumped into his bag, did it?' said Billie.

Georgie winced. 'OK, it *is* his fault. But you won't mind when you know why. He wasn't doing anything awful. He was— Well, you tell them, Edmond.'

Edmond Hudson's shoulders slumped, and he fussed with his bow tie. 'It's not for me. It's for Domino. My pig.'

'Your *pig*?' said Sam.

'They make really good pets,' said Edmond sadly. 'I know most people have cats or dogs or rabbits, but if they knew how friendly pigs were, then everyone would want one. Only – she does take up a bit of space. And she eats lots of food. And, um . . .' He looked at Georgie.

'Edmond lives with his grandparents. Only they've had to move into a new flat so that his grandad doesn't have to do any stairs, and he's not allowed animals there. So – his granny said he had to get rid of her, or . . . or she'd put Domino in the oven and eat her for dinner.'

Sam gasped. Billie covered her mouth with her hands.

I tried to imagine someone saying that about Spooky – which didn't really work because people

251

don't eat cats the way they eat bacon. But I could imagine someone trying to get rid of him. He wouldn't like it. He would mew and quiver and need to be wrapped up in a blanket and fed Dreamies.

Edmond blew his nose on a hankie from his pocket.

'Sandy and Cam, my old next-door neighbours, said I could keep her in their garden if I came to feed her every day. Pigs really like leftovers! So I've been doing that. But Granny kept noticing that food was going missing, and she mostly buys frozen lasagne and Rich Tea biscuits anyway. I didn't want to steal, I promise! I never took from the same lunch box two days in a row. And I always left enough food behind for it to still be a nice lunch – or I tried to. But – then you put blue stuff in it, and I didn't know if it was safe for her to eat, so for a few days I couldn't give her anything . . .'

'Do pigs leave bite marks in people's apples?' asked Billie slowly.

Edmond's cheeks went pale. 'No. That was me. Granny – she forgets things. Like dinner, sometimes. Or that I live there too. So – it wasn't always for Domino. Sometimes it was for me.' He wrapped his arms even more tightly around the satchel, looking very small and sad.

I gave him a fish finger. I didn't really know what else to do.

He held it awkwardly in his hand.

'It was wrong. I'm a thief. It doesn't matter why I did it. It's still a crime. Call the police. I'll go quietly.'

'I'm not calling the police to my birthday party,' said Sam.

'We're not calling the police at all!' said Georgie.

'Course not,' I said.

'Though – maybe someone ought to know about your granny,' said Billie gently.

Edmond nodded. 'Yes, please. I think – I think someone should. But you won't tell them about the pig?'

We all promised.

Sam went to have a quiet and careful word with Dr Paget, who was good at mending families, and she came and had a private little chat with Edmond.

At the end of the party Dr Skidelsky let out a yelp of dismay. 'Where's the football cake? Gen? Did it get chopped up already?'

'Oh dear, what a shame,' said Sam in an odd robotic voice.

'Wherever can it have got to?' said Billie.

'Such a pity,' I said.

We made sure no one looked too closely at Edmond Hudson's satchel.

'That was so kind of you,' Georgie said to Sam on the way out. 'I'm not sure I could be that kind.'

'Nah, it's fine,' said Sam. 'It was courgette cake under all that icing. It's the worst cake in the whole world. I bet the pig will love it.'

GEORGIE

'Right, lads,' said Joel on Sunday morning after Bridget had dropped the Magees home. 'We are having a family day. Me and Mina . . . we had a little chat . . .'

Mum coughed. 'What he means is, we had an argument.'

Jem stiffened on the blue sofa beside me. 'Nope! No, you didn't! Not on V-Day! You're not allowed to have arguments at all, ever, and especially not then.'

'I think you'll find that we are, and we will again,' said Mum.

Noah sighed heavily. Tilly lay face-down on the floor.

Jem threw me a panicky look.

'But they made up again afterwards – didn't you?' I said hopefully, scooping Spooky onto my lap.

'Sure we did,' said Joel, wrapping his arm round Mum's shoulder and kissing her ear.

Mum smiled softly. 'Actually, it was a very useful argument, as they sometimes are. Joel pointed out that sometimes I might put work first—'

'All the time, I think I said?'

'Yes, and I disagreed with you, darling.'

'Stop it!' Jem scrunched up into a ball on the sofa and put her hands over her ears.

I looked pleadingly at Mum.

She rolled her eyes, and then she smiled again. 'I do work long hours. It's what I do. But I don't want it to become something that hurts my family. I know I've hurt you sometimes, Georgie, by not putting you first.'

I put my face in Spooky's fur so I wouldn't have to look at anyone while I was quite so blushy.

'And I've already done that with you, Jem, letting you down with our plans when we've only just started getting to know each other.'

Jem unfurled, just a little.

'I can't promise I'll always be perfect. Especially if a lorry full of furniture polish decides to crash itself again . . .' She paused, tapping her phone anxiously. Then she coughed and put it in her pocket. 'But I have a beautiful family – a new family – and we aren't spending anything like enough time together. For a variety of reasons.' She gave Joel a pointy look. 'So – I thought it would be lovely to have a family day. The first of many, I hope. Doing something *together.*'

She clutched Joel's hand with both of hers, and I felt a warm glowy feeling all over.

Jem beamed at me and sat up straight. 'Can we design a new logo for Fairy Dusters? Because me and Martin think you need a new one.'

'Lloyd Park! Frisbee golf!' shouted Noah.

'The London Dungeon,' said Tilly, from the floor.

'There's those cable cars over the river,' said Joel slowly. 'I've always wanted to give them a go.'

'Oh,' said Mum. 'I was thinking of a nice stroll through somewhere shoppy, with lovely stalls of lovely things. Covent Garden, or Borough Market.'

'It's meant to be something that all of us'll like, love,' said Joel gently.

'Who doesn't like Covent Garden?'

Noah put his hand up.

'Do you know what Covent Garden is, Nono?' I asked gently.

'I know what it isn't, and it isn't Lloyd Park and frisbee golf.'

'We went there yesterday!' said Jem.

'So?'

The doorbell rang, which was a bit of a relief, even though it made Spooky's claws sink into my knees.

'I'll go,' I said, shooing the cat away.

There were two unfamiliar girls on the doorstep: one smallish, about Tilly's size, with light brown skin and curly brown hair in braided rows all over her head; one older than me, very pale, her red curls in a ponytail. She looked quite anxious. The small one, however, looked furious.

'My name is Tinkerbell,' she said, improbably. 'This is my sister Pea,' she added, also improbably.

'Like the vegetable,' said the red-headed girl reluctantly, as if it was a thing she had to explain a lot. 'We live over the road. Next door to the Paget-Skidelskys?'

'Oh! You've got a dog too,' I said, remembering New Year's Eve.

'Yes, and you've got a dad who comes outdoors in his pants,' she said, visibly regretting saying so as the words came out of her mouth.

I liked her. She seemed a lot like me.

'Never mind all that! What are you going to do about *this*?' demanded Tinkerbell, thrusting a pile of torn pink cardboard into my hands.

It was one of Tilly and Noah's valentine cards, now shredded. I could just about make out pieces of the name *Tinkerbell* picked out in blue glitter.

'Are you cross because someone gave you a valentine?' I asked, confused.

'Yes!' she said, stamping her foot. 'Stupid Angelo. Who I don't even like. But I said I'd be his girlfriend because he sent me this, and Clover says I'm old enough for holding hands – she's my other sister – and now it turns out he sent one to six other people! Who are all his girlfriend now too!'

'That doesn't sound very practical,' I said.

'That's what *I* said!' said Pea. 'One for every day of the week. When you'd want weekends off, really.'

259

I nodded; I thought so too. 'Well, I'm sorry. That doesn't sound much fun. But I think you ought to be being cross with Angelo, not us.'

'That's what I said,' whispered Pea.

Tinkerbell stared up at her mutinously.

'And we can't give you your money back because you ripped it up,' I added, feeling less certain.

'I said that too,' whispered Pea. 'Come on, Tink. Let's make Angelo an *I Don't Want to Be Your Girlfriend* card. I don't think anywhere sells those. Which is odd, isn't it? Nice to meet you, anyway. Maybe see you again? Bye!'

And she tugged her sister away, while she grumbled about the general meanness of the universe.

When I got back, they were all still arguing over where to go on a fun family day out.

'Enough!' I said loudly. 'This isn't familyish at all. And it's obvious we all want to do different things, and we'll never agree, so there's no sense arguing. Everyone, write your name on a slip of paper – then we'll pick one out and do whatever that person wants to do. And we'll keep all the slips, and next time someone else will have their turn. Any objections?'

'Blimey,' said Tilly. 'You have got good at being a big sister.'

'Hasn't she just,' said Mum in a proud voice, climbing off the sofa to wrap me in a hug. 'You're blossoming, darling! You really are!'

It was very embarrassing, but also a bit nice.

We let Noah pick out the first piece of paper. It said, *This is Noah but we should do whatever Georgie wants to do because it was her idea*, which nearly made me cry.

'Hairdos!' said Tilly.

'In leotards!' said Noah.

'Georgie's pick, remember!' said Joel.

'Um,' I said, because suddenly it was hard to think of things I wanted. 'Oh! Wait here.'

I dashed upstairs and hunted under my bed. Then I came back down holding a battered old oblong box.

'Cluedo?' said Mum. 'Where did that come from?'

'Granny. She gave it to me ages ago. She said you loved it when you were little. Only – well, you need more than two people to play it anyway.'

Mum gave me a hug again, this time a very long tight one, with kisses on top of my head.

It turned out to be quite difficult to play Cluedo with Magees. Noah decided he was called Professor Bum, and he and Tilly collapsed into giggles every time he was suspected. Some of the murder weapons had gone missing out of the old box, and had to be swapped for nearby objects, which meant Dr Black might have been killed by a giraffe with a wonky leg instead of some lead piping. And the card for the conservatory had a big rip in it, so everyone knew Jem had it, and she got grumpy.

Usually I only liked games when people were sensible and played by the proper rules. But I loved Giraffe Cluedo even more than the usual sort. Maybe Mum was right. I was blossoming.

Afterwards we went to Queen's Park for a walk, and Mum cooked us spaghetti for dinner: the real kind, with no courgettes. We all watched *Brave* together, and sang along. Then Tilly and Noah went to bed.

Me and Jem sat on the stairs, listening to Mum and Joel being all giggly on the sofa.

'I like it when they don't argue,' she said.

'Me too.'

'Georgie – they won't ever split up, will they?'

'Um. Well, hopefully not. But we'd still be sisters even if they did.'

'Superglue sisters,' said Jem thoughtfully.

Then she hopped up, went into the kitchen and made us all hot cocoa, with sprinkles on the top.

'No!' she said when I went to pick up the nearest mug. 'Not that one!'

'They're all the same, Jem.'

'Um. Course they are. But this one that is the same is yours.' She pushed a different mug towards me, and then carried two others very carefully into the back room, and handed one to Joel, and then one to Mum. Then she stood awkwardly in a corner, watching and waiting until they'd both finished.

I drank mine very slowly and suspiciously, just in case there was anything in it that might stop me getting boobies. Now I was blossoming, I didn't want to stop.

JEM

Dear 7E,
   USS are doing brilliantly at finding out who all the secrets belong to but there are two left.

   ~~Lunch-box thief~~ EDMOND HUDSON
   ~~Curly fries~~ ALFIE
   Secret chess wizard
   Never kissed anyone
   ~~Goldfish murderer~~ MADISON
   ~~Scared of bees~~ NISHAT

   Feel free to hurry up and tell us who you are so we can de-volcano you.

From Jemima Magee, aged 11¼

On Monday Mr Miller had a mystery on his desk. It was large and knobbly, with a red cloth hanging over it.

'Is it a bird in a cage, sir?' asked Big Mohammad.

'Can we eat it?' called Alfie. 'Is it a coffee machine?'

'Is it Miss Eagle's foot?' asked Halid.

'Ew, gross,' said Madison, pinging a pencil at his head.

'Yes, all right,' drawled Mr Miller, yawning. 'It isn't any of those. It's something much more . . . Oh God, who invented Mondays . . .? Where was I? Oh. Something . . . exciting.' He yawned again. 'Congratulations . . . to, er . . . Hang on, I wrote it down . . . To the winner of the Hedgewick and Webley Cup and Junior Regional Champion Chess Master for the South-east . . . Efe Okoye.'

He pulled back the red cloth to reveal a shiny silver cup with ribbons on the handles and Efe's name engraved on a square of gold at the base.

Efe made a squeaking noise and wrapped her arms round her head.

'No way!' said Sam. '*You're* the secret chess wizard?'

She nodded, peeking out between her fingers. 'That's what I was talking to Mrs Cooper about, the day Miss Eagle broke her ankle. We played. I won. Three times. Then she signed me up for a sort of chess club on weekends. Sorry.'

'Don't be sorry!' said Billie, prodding her. 'That's amazing! My brother's got loads of trophies and stuff from rugby. I'd love to win a cup like that. Something really massive. Massiver than any of his.'

'You don't think chess is boring?' Efe whispered. 'You will still be friends with a chess person?'

'Of course we're still friends,' said Georgie kindly. 'You should be really proud.'

Then Mr Miller put the red cloth over his head and went to sleep.

'I don't know what Miss Eagle sees in him,' sighed Billie at lunch time. 'She's all soft and kind and wears pretty clothes, and he's . . .'

'A gitwizard,' said Sam. 'With a stupid beard. I wouldn't go out with him if he was the last boy in the entire universe.'

'He's a teacher,' said Efe seriously. 'That is not allowed.'

'Imagine kissing him, and feeling his hairy face tickling your chin,' said Georgie, screwing up her face.

We all giggled.

'At least we know *he* didn't put the never-kissed-anyone secret in the secrets ball,' said Billie.

Suddenly everyone looked vaguely guilty.

Except for Georgie, who just looked thoughtful.

'It's a bit strange, don't you think,' she said slowly, 'how all those secrets got put up on the wall . . .? But not mine. Or yours, Billie.'

Billie swallowed her bite of pastry in one awkward gulp.

'Unless one of you's the never-kissed-anyone person,' said Sam, laughing.

Billie stuck out her tongue. 'I've never kissed anyone. Not like girlfriendy-boyfriendy kissing. But that's not a secret.'

'Nor me,' said Georgie quietly.

But her eyes stayed fixed on Billie's.

I could tell she was thinking something. She has a particular crinkle just above her nose when she is working out a puzzle that probably only I know about. I just didn't know what the puzzle was.

'Well, it's not Madison who's never kissed anyone,' said Sam firmly. 'She never talks about anything else. Once Mrs Cox-Patel put us together in Maths doing pie charts, and she made ours about the relative sexy fitness of all the boys. Apparently only six per cent of the class got Top Sexy marks – which turned out to just be Paolo. Mrs Cox-Patel said it was a brilliant example of data that should not be represented as a pie chart.'

I opened my mouth to say that actually Madison's secret was being a goldfish murderer – but I caught Georgie's eye and turned it into half a sneeze.

'Is she going to do make-up for the play, like Lianne said?' asked Billie.

And then they got sucked into talking about a lot of boring MEEE stuff.

Georgie stayed late after school to do more MEEE planning with Mrs Bianco, the Drama teacher, who was running the whole Easter Extravaganza.

At home I found Noah lying flat on one of the benches hugging a cushion; the blue one off the sofa.

'Did you get any valentines, Nono?' I asked.

'I'm six,' he said, blinking at me solemnly.

'Fair enough. Shall I fetch Doris Morris to cheer you up?'

Noah gulped, and then buried his face in the cushion and sobbed.

'Boys,' said Tilly, shaking her head as she wandered past. 'So over-emotional.'

Georgie was a bit over-excited when she came home.

'It's going to be so amazing!' she said, bouncing on my bed. 'We're on stage near the end, after all the orchestra and poetry and readings and things, which is basically the best slot in the whole Extravaganza. And Miss Eagle is definitely coming and she doesn't know a thing about it! A complete secret! Oh – and this is best of all. I've worked out how to find our last volcano person and give them back an ordinary internal mountain – and help find more people to be in the play, all at the same time!'

It sounded a lot more MEEE than USS, but I smiled anyway because she looked so happy.

'OK. How?'

'Well, the only secret we haven't worked out yet is the never-kissed-anyone secret, and there's still a few people it could be: Big Mohammad, or that girl Acacia who sits at the back and never says anything. Or Billie. Or maybe someone put in two secrets! Anyway, my idea will help everyone.'

She beamed, and produced the Hogwarty Shakespeare book. I made a little groany noise, but she shushed me.

'In the play there are these four lovers who get lost in the forest because they keep arguing. And the fairies – no, listen, honestly – they give them a love potion to make them fall in love again. Puck carries it about in a flower, and drips it into their eyes.'

I gave her a stern look. 'I'm not making a love potion.'

'No, you won't have to!'

'Good. Because love potions don't even work like that. Dripping it into people's eyes – honestly . . . that Shakespeare was useless.'

Georgie looked cross. 'Jem, shush up about your silly magic stuff a minute. This is important.'

'It's not silly,' I mumbled, grinding one foot into the floor.

Georgie sighed. 'OK. Sorry. Anyway – what we're going to do is make a *stage* potion. Like, a made-up bottle of any old stuff. We'll put glitter in it so that it looks magic.'

I made a growly noise.

'Just for the play! And then we'll get Big Mohammad and Acacia and Billie, and anyone else we can think of, to come to a special audition – and we'll tell them you made the potion because everyone believes you're a real witch.'

I made a louder growly noise.

'Which you are! But it's important they believe in it, because then they'll all kiss each other! And then they'll all have been kissed – not just for a play, but really! And all the secrets will be fixed!'

'Do what now?' said Dad, stumbling into my bedroom wrapped in Mina's silky dressing gown, with his hair sticking up and one eye shut.

'Oops,' said Georgie. 'Were we being a bit loud?'

'For a fella on the night shift you were, kiddo.' He cracked open the other eye, rubbing it as he perched on the window seat. 'What was that about everyone kissing each other?'

271

Georgie smiled. 'Well . . .' She explained it again – missing out a few details, like the hamster and Edmond Hudson's pig.

Dad blinked a lot. Then he folded his arms and shook his head sadly.

'I don't know where you got the idea that was all right, girls,' he said, as if I had anything to do with it, 'but you can't go making people kiss each other. That's not OK.'

'But it's for a good cause!' said Georgie. 'Everyone who has a secret like that is carrying it about like a – a personal volcano! And we're helping to make it go *poof*!'

'Are you?' said Dad, scrunching up his face. 'Seems to me you're making people do something they wouldn't choose to. So someone told you – told somebody, anyway – they'd never kissed anyone. They didn't say they wanted to. They didn't say that at all. You're talking like they need help – but they never asked for it.'

'But . . . fixing things is what we do,' I mumbled.

'This doesn't need fixing. Nothing's broken. So nothing needs fixing.' Dad rubbed his eyes again.

'You leave those poor folk alone, eh? Just you leave them be.'

And he padded away, sighing, to make himself some coffee.

'He doesn't understand,' said Georgie, staring down at the book, all subdued.

'Not at all,' I said.

'We were being nice,' said Georgie.

'Super nice,' I said.

But a horrible grumbling feeling in my insides told me that he might be right, just a little bit. And I didn't like it at all.

MARCH

GEORGIE

'How's my blossomer?' asked Mum, tiptoeing into my bedroom with a cup of soothing camomile tea.

'A bit wilty,' I said, cuddling my pillow.

It was the night before the Easter Extravaganza. One more sleep. Assuming I *could* sleep. I was much more likely to spend all night staring at the ceiling, imagining all the ways it could be a disaster.

Jem had finally been persuaded to join MEEE and help sew all the costumes – but there were still six sets of wings to sew onto T-shirts.

Nishat had decided she would only be a tree if she could be one with her back to the audience.

Halid wouldn't stand next to any of the fairies.

Still absolutely no one was willing to play the part of Bottom, so it was a donkey head nailed on the end of a broom, and Jem shouting the lines from offstage.

And at the end I had to do a dance in front of everyone. It had a very ankle-twisty section in the middle that I was quite confident would send me off to hospital, just like Miss Eagle.

Worst of all – if any of it went wrong, it would be all my fault.

'You'll be wonderful, my darling,' said Mum, kissing my hair. 'And I'll be the proudest mum in the whole audience, just you wait.'

I felt quite sick when she switched off the light.

I listened to all the noises of the house as everyone else went to bed. I counted sheep, then sheep in ballet shoes, then sheep with donkey heads on.

Then I heard creaky floorboards and whispering below.

As I crept down the stairs, and down again, I heard low voices from the kitchen.

'Let me! I have more puff.'

'You're mean.'

'I'm not mean, I'm nine. People often mix those up.'

There was a strange sound of deep breaths, then a squeaky noise.

'It's not going to work.'

'It *is* going to work, Nono. It will just take ages because you're being annoying.'

There was another series of big breaths, and a groan.

'What *are* you doing?' I asked, pushing the kitchen door open.

Tilly and Noah both yelped and leaped backwards.

'Nothing,' said Tilly, hiding something behind her back.

There was an open plastic packet on the table. TWENTY PARTY BALLOONS. MAKE YOUR BIRTHDAY PARTY GO WITH A BANG.

'Whose birthday is it?'

'Um,' said Noah.

'Probably lots of people's,' said Tilly, pushing her hair off her face. 'I mean, every day must be. Could you blow up this balloon, please? Because it looks easy, but actually it is impossible.'

She thrust a golden balloon with HAPPY 60TH BIRTHDAY printed on it towards me.

I gave it a little stretch, then blew it up in four big puffs, tied a knot in the end and presented it to her. 'Shall I do the rest?'

'No,' they both said. And they walked off happily together and went straight to bed.

Breakfast was hopeless.

'I'll have your toast,' said Jem helpfully, taking it off my plate and nibbling round the edges strangely. 'And then I'll send you my energy.' She wiggled her fingers.

'Can we come?' asked Noah.

'Not in the middle of the school day,' said Mum sternly.

'She'll do an extra performance this evening, just for you,' Jem promised.

Assuming I didn't break my ankle . . . or fall off the stage . . . or just dissolve into a puddle of utter terror . . .

'You are definitely coming, Mum?' I asked as she pulled my polar-bear hat onto my head.

'Of course, darling,' she said.

Then her phone rang, and she disappeared into her office before she remembered to wish me good luck.

*

The whole morning passed in a fog of queasy panic.

'I'll be leaving at lunch time to collect her,' said Mr Miller, who was wearing his best cardigan with the leather patches on the elbows and one of those ties made of wool that looks like a sock. 'Eleanor. Miss Eagle. She said she doesn't need a lift, but I don't want her overdoing it. She is so passionate . . . so high-spirited . . .'

'Is she definitely coming to watch us?' asked Big Mohammad.

'Is she excited, sir?' asked Halid.

'She said she's missed you all, though I don't know why. And she has no idea what she's coming to see. All a surprise!'

Everyone was excited. None of the teachers minded that I hadn't done my homework about contour lines, even though I always, always did my homework on time, or that I spent all netball practising my spins, which was not very Goal Attack of me at all.

After lunch everyone went back to lessons, except for those in the Extravaganza, to give us time for a dress rehearsal in the sports-complex hall.

It was very big. And very echoey. There was a low stage at the front, and opposite it, rows and rows of seats, on a rake like in a theatre, so that nearly two hundred people would be able to sit down.

'I'm just not going to think about that,' said Sam, who was being Oberon, King of the Fairies, and was almost as nervous as me.

First up was the orchestra, so I had to be in that.

Agnieska Milinska from 7B did a traditional dance.

Oliver Box played the trombone.

Then there was a poetry section from Year 8, which was very slow and mumbly.

We were on next.

'Miss, I just need to make sure everyone is here—' I said, looking around anxiously for Jem, who had promised me that all the costumes would absolutely be ready by now.

Then there was a *pop*, and all the lights went out.

'Sorry!' called Mrs Bianco from the darkness. 'Think I might have plugged in one too many lamps! You've rehearsed it through, right, Georgie?

Good girl. Sure it'll be fine. Back here in thirty minutes, everyone! Have a wee! Eat chocolate! Break a leg!'

I stumbled off the stage in darkness and sat on a stool, tucked behind a curtain.

'It'll be fine . . . She's sure it'll be fine . . . It'll all be fine . . .' I whispered to myself, to calm down the flutteriness inside.

There was a small rustly noise.

'Sorry!' whispered Billie, emerging from behind another curtain. 'I – um – hello.'

I sniffed. 'Hello.'

She smiled at me very awkwardly. Then she sat on the floor and nibbled on her fingernail.

'I have to tell you something,' she said. 'I've been meaning to tell you for ages, only . . . well, I wasn't sure how. Or if I should. But . . .' She took a deep breath. 'I know your secret, Georgie.'

All my nervy worries about dancing in front of Miss Eagle fell away – overwhelmed by a huge crashy wave of new ones.

'It was *you*!' I whispered, my voice coming out wobbly. 'I knew it! *You* stole the secrets ball and *you* put them all on the wall!'

I'd been thinking it for ages, and not knowing how not to be her friend any more.

Billie's mouth fell open. 'No. I would never – not ever!' She looked wounded. 'I don't know who it was. But – well, I found this in my dad's office, and, um . . . I could sort of guess.'

She reached into her backpack and pulled out a furled copy of *Business Trader Weekly.*

The one with a smiling picture of Mum on the front, holding up the Fairy Dusters logo. The one from four years ago, when she'd just started to make it big. The one with the interview.

'There's an interview inside . . .'

'I know what it says,' I said, my voice coming out dull. I felt heavy all over.

McKay's route to business success hasn't all been sprinkled with fairy dust. Her first venture, undertaken with her former husband, was a building finance company. When the relationship turned abusive, McKay struggled to accept it. 'I wanted us to be the perfect happy couple everyone thought we were. It was incredibly hard to walk away from the life we'd made. But the day he hit me in front of our daughter was the day I walked out. Directly to the police station.' McKay fought a fierce public battle to gain the rights to the company – only to discover that the business was mired in fraudulent debt, and quite worthless. 'I hit rock bottom. He'd taken everything from me: our home, our safety, and now everything we'd worked for. I couldn't let him get away with it. I have a beautiful daughter. She deserves to grow up in a world where the bad guys are punished and the right side wins.' And win she certainly did with Fairy Dusters, begun with a small business loan and now selling franchises across Europe. Her ex, meanwhile, is serving a sentence at Her Majesty's Pleasure.

'I had to ask my dad what that meant,' said Billie, sitting down beside me.

'He's in prison. My dad used to hurt my mum. And then he went to prison.' I wanted to cry but my throat felt hollow. Nothing came out.

'That was your secret?'

I nodded. Then I shut my eyes because I could feel her looking at me and the shamefulness of it all was just too much.

'That is definitely Hidden Depths,' she said conversationally. 'It doesn't make you a bad person, though – you know that, right? Just unlucky with dads. Lots of people are.'

I nodded.

'Do you miss him?'

Then I *did* cry – because no one ever asks that, and I do. I really do. I wish I didn't. But I do.

'I know he was awful,' I sobbed. 'He was awful to my mum. And he said horrible things in court. And we are better off without him. But . . . there were times when he wasn't awful. I miss those.'

Billie wrapped me up in a hug and let me cry on her jumper for as long as I wanted.

Then she gave me one of her sparkly smiles and said, 'Guess what . . . I didn't put my secret in the secrets ball, after all. I just pretended to. But I'm going to tell you because it's only fair, and I want to.'

She whispered it into my ear.

I felt my eyes go wide, even though I tried not to look too shocked. It was a big secret. Just as big as mine.

'I won't tell anyone, ever,' I promised.

'Me too,' she said.

The volcano didn't magically turn into just an internal mountain, exactly. But now that Billie had shared her secret, I felt like I would always want to be kind to her, even though, if I was really a good person, I should already think that. I trusted her. She trusted me. And that feeling wasn't like a volcano. It was like a little bonfire, right in my heart, keeping me warm.

'Stay here – tell Mrs Bianco I'll be back really soon,' I said.

I had to tell Jem. She was the only other person who knew. She was the only one who would understand.

I jumped off the stage and weaved my way through the chairs in the dark to the girls' changing rooms.

EXTRAVAGANZA DRESSING ROOM
KNOCK FIRST - PEOPLE MIGHT
BE IN THEIR PANTS

said the sign on the door.

By this point I had seen a lot of people in their pants, and I reckoned my bonfire was more important anyway – so I didn't knock. I just pushed open the door.

Jem was the only one there.

She wasn't sewing costumes.

She wasn't learning her lines.

She was crouching over a small pile of paper slips, nestled in the cracked shell of a shiny green papier-mâché post box.

JEM

Dear Georgie,
   I'm sorry. Really really sorry. I didn't put your secret up. I would never have done that. It was very brave of you to put it in there. You're really brave all over.
   Really really really sorry.

From Jemima Magee, aged 11½

So what happened back on that Friday afternoon, ages ago, is: when Miss Eagle fell off the step and broke her ankle, the secrets ball went *bounce, bounce, bounce* down the steps, and rolled past all the people going 'Oh no!' and 'Help!' and 'Urgh, miss, your foot is pointing the wrong way!' and stopped at me.

Right at my feet.

You can't ignore that sort of thing. It's like fate, which is basically magic for everyone.

Obviously I picked it up and put it in my bag, and I was completely going to give it back or set fire to it or something. Until I thought about it properly. Until I realized we could fix things.

But when I explained all that here in the changing rooms, Georgie didn't understand at all.

'How *could* you? How? Why? You lied and lied and let us all think . . . and worry . . . Oh, Jem, I don't think I can ever forgive you.'

I felt a bit sideways then, because Georgie doesn't say things she doesn't mean.

'No, but – listen, Georgie. I did it for good reasons. So you can't be cross. And now lots of things are fixed because everyone's secrets have come out. Unhappy people have got hamsters. Ariadne doesn't have to only say *Bof.* I saved up the ones that I thought were really upsetting! I wouldn't have shared yours, I promise!'

Georgie's mouth opened, then shut again. 'Why not?' she whispered.

'Because . . . it would make you sad. Because you asked me not to.'

I felt sideways again.

'But, Jem – everyone felt like that about their secret. Everyone would've asked you not to. And you just didn't care.'

'I *did* care.'

I cared loads. I always care loads. I wouldn't have done any of it if I didn't.

'I wonder,' said a voice from behind the wall of lockers, 'if now might be the best time to announce myself.'

There was an odd noise – not footsteps exactly, but a rhythmic clicky tapping – and Miss Eagle came round the lockers into the changing room, supporting herself on her crutches.

'Um. How long . . .?' I mumbled.

'Long enough, I think,' she said, sitting awkwardly on a bench and putting her crutches down beside her. She was wearing a deep-green dress with little chicks printed on it, and one red shoe; her other foot was encased in a black foam boot now, instead of a cast. 'I just came in to put on a little make-up before wishing everyone luck. Mrs Cooper told me you had a little something planned. But I think I might be needed here first, hmm?'

I could see Georgie looking at the clock and noticing it was only five minutes until the Extravaganza, which is just *so* Georgie. But Miss Eagle didn't look like she planned on going anywhere.

'First, I think I should apologize,' she said. 'I thought it would be a positive, emotionally uplifting exercise to write down the secrets and set them free. I should've realized it might not be quite so simple.'

'It's not your fault, miss,' murmured Georgie.

They both waited and looked at me.

'I'm not going to say sorry. I'm *not* sorry. I was fixing things. I was bringing good into the world! You don't understand!'

Miss Eagle tilted her head to one side. 'If it was all for the good, why didn't you tell anyone, Jem? Why was sharing all the secrets a secret itself?'

That was easy. ''Cos it was fun. Like a treasure hunt. And – to help you, Georgie. Because then you had a good way to make friends, with all your organizing and planning and all the USS things, and everyone would like you. I was being nice. I was helping.'

'Hmm,' said Miss Eagle. 'I'm not sure Georgie really needs any help with making friends, does she? I haven't known either of you very long, but she seems more than competent at it to me. She's put this play together almost single-handed.' She smoothed down her skirt. 'I wonder how that feels if you're used to being in charge. Making all the decisions, controlling your world . . . and then finding that it's not so easy after all. Perhaps you hoped all this might help *you* make friends, Jemima.'

'No – Jem's really good at that, miss,' said Georgie. 'She sort of does it for both of us.'

I nodded because it was true. It's always been true.

But Miss Eagle kept looking at me with her head tilted to one side, and my insides went wriggly.

I suppose I *was* a bit fed up that whenever I had visitation with my mum, Georgie went off to do fun things with Billie and Sam, when she is supposed to be *my* best friend, not anyone else's.

Tilly and Noah liked her as well. Probably more than me, actually, because she's less shouty and can do hairdos.

Even Dad didn't need me as much, now that he had a Mina.

Or Mum.

And I wasn't jealous, obviously. I'm totally fine all by myself doing my crafts and my magic and having good sparkly Jemmish thoughts – because I'm interesting enough for at least two people. Maybe two and a half. But it's better when there are other people around to be impressed.

Maybe I *was* jealous. A tiny bit.

Maybe sometimes it would be nice *not* to be interesting or quirky or a unique sparkly gem.

Miss Eagle took a deep breath, then glanced at the clock and pushed herself back onto her foot, resting on her crutches.

'You know, the thing with secrets that you got right, Jem, is that it can help to share them. But only if and when you freely choose to. Only if you trust the person you share them with. Sometimes sharing them can set you free – from your past . . . from guilt . . .

'I wonder,' she said, clicking towards the door. She paused beside the hollow cracked curve of the broken shiny green ball, gazing down at the last few slips. 'All that wanting to fix things . . . I wonder what would set *you* free.'

Miss Eagle turned and stared meaningfully into my eyes.

Then she clicked away.

I looked at the slips of paper and swallowed hard. Now I knew for definite: Miss Eagle had totally read all the secrets. And even if she didn't know my handwriting very well, she knew which one was mine.

I felt a crawly feeling all over my skin. An awful, guilty, sicky worry that grew through me like roots and settled heavily in my stomach like an old potato.

And then I realized – that was what Georgie had felt all along. What everyone with secrets had felt.

And I'd made it happen with my stupid secrets plan.

'I'm sorry – I'm so sorry,' I whispered.

Georgie gasped. 'Oh, Jem, what is it? Are you—?'

She stepped forward, then hesitated, remembering she was meant to be never forgiving me for ever.

It felt horrible. Knowing that she was right there, and that I didn't deserve her as a friend at all.

'Here,' I said, reaching into the cracked ball and tugging out a square of paper, folded in half. 'You should read this.'

'No, Jem, I don't *want* to read anyone else's – weren't you listening at all?!'

'It's mine. I lied. I *did* have a secret.'

Her eyes shot wide.

I pressed the paper into her hand. 'I give you my permission. I want you to read it. I trust you.'

I could hardly breathe as she unfolded the paper, a little frown creasing her eyebrows as she read. She narrowed her eyes, reading it again.

Then she threw back her head and laughed out loud.

'What?' I said, snatching the paper back, suddenly panicked that I'd given her the wrong one. But no. It was my secret looking back at me.

I am a real witch with magic powers like Hermione Granger in 'Harry Potter', only better. I can control people and make things happen. I made my dad fall in love with my best friend's mum using a magic love potion because I wanted us to live together. Only now I'm scared that if it goes wrong it'll all be my fault.

'What?' I said again, stamping my foot this time as Georgie smirked.

'Oh, you big nana,' she said, giving me a hug. 'Have you really been worried about that all this time? *You* didn't make them fall in love. There's no magic potion that can make that happen – especially not with my mum. No one in the world is ever going to make her do anything she doesn't want to. Trust me.'

'No, but – I *did* make it happen! They got together – and then they had that big fight in Nando's about who was paying the bill for butterfly chicken and macho peas – you remember – and they were going to break up, and Mum said I should wave my magic wand and get them back together if I was so upset about it. So I did! I did a million spells to make them be in love. Whenever I came to your house I put three drips of magic in Mina's coffee. And scrolls in Dad's pockets with magic words written on in invisible ink. And glitter under Mina's pillow – because actually glitter can be magic if you bless it properly. For weeks and weeks. And then . . . it worked. My magic really *worked*. For the first time ever. That's how I knew I properly was a witch.'

Before that I just had a black cat, and a mum with pocketfuls of crystals and a bat tattoo. After that I had *powers*.

Georgie tilted her head, smiling. 'Or . . . perhaps . . . you wanted something. A lot. And it happened. But not because of you.' She pressed her lips together, looking apologetic. 'Maybe you aren't really a witch, Jem,' she said gently. 'Maybe you'd just like to be able to control things. But I don't think anyone can do that. I don't think anyone should be able to.'

I could see what she was saying because it is a big responsibility. And it sort of needs me to get everything right on behalf of other people, when maybe I could let them find out what's right for themselves. Even if they get it wrong sometimes and fight in chicken restaurants.

But if that was true, then everything I liked about me would crumble all to bits.

My funny clothes.

My crystals.

Me and my mum and our special grown-up time that was just for us.

'If I'm not a witch, I'm just a weirdo,' I said, my voice coming out small.

Georgie smiled. 'I like weirdos.'

She gave me a hug. I reckoned that meant she had forgiven me after all.

'Honestly. Your dad isn't under a love spell. He's not wandering around like he's got a donkey head on. He's just— Oh! The play!'

She leaped back, looking at the clock – as the changing-room door flew open, and Halid and Big Mohammad and all the others began to file in, looking for their costumes.

'I haven't finished,' I squeaked, jumping up in front of the bench to hide the evidence of my crimes. 'We're not ready!'

'Yes, we are,' said Georgie firmly. 'Come on in.'

When I spun round, she had already tucked the broken shiny green ball and the last slips of paper away in my school bag.

'But—' I whispered.

She smiled. 'Like Miss Eagle said. *Your* secret. So *you* choose to tell people – or not.' Then she turned away. 'Right – does everyone know their cue? Fairies, line up by the mirrors for pixie dusting! Nishat, practise being a tree! Alfie, why is there a hamster in the donkey head? Places, everyone – quick quick quick!'

GEORGIE

I didn't break my ankle, or fall off the stage, or dissolve into a puddle of terror.

I watched from the wings as Sam strode about, tripping over her cloak, and, due to an unfortunate mishap involving inadequate hammering from Efe, the donkey head rolled across the stage and Billie had to kiss a broom handle. Everyone was still laughing when I danced on in my Puck costume, which was a white T-shirt and white leggings with talc in my hair.

I didn't do it perfectly. I wobbled a lot, and the talc kept coming off in clouds, and someone in the audience was shining a bright light in my face, which was distracting. But I danced it quite well, actually. Without dying. In front of people. And everyone clapped and clapped and wouldn't stop for ages.

Miss Eagle was at the front, and she had to dab at her face with a tissue.

I looked out across the rest of the crowd and saw where the light had been coming from: Martin, recording it on his iPad.

My heart did a sinking thing because I knew what that meant.

But then I saw Joel next to him, beaming so proudly his face looked like a big round moon in the dark, and my heart bobbed right back up.

'Oh, well done, well done!' said Miss Eagle, gathering us all together outside the sports complex after the Extravaganza had finished. 'I couldn't have dreamed up anything more wonderful myself. Thank you.'

'They had quite a bit of help, you know,' said Mr Miller, shuffling Efe out of the way to stand next to her, and puffing his chest out. 'From, uh, yours truly.' He fiddled with his sock tie.

'No, we didn't,' said Sam.

'You were completely useless,' said Billie.

'He's a rubbish boyfriend, miss,' said Big Mohammad.

'Oh dear, Simon,' said Miss Eagle, frowning at him as if he was a very naughty Year 7. 'What have you been telling them?'

And it turned out that he wasn't her boyfriend at all – he just wanted to be. Except he hadn't asked, and she hadn't said yes, so it wasn't all right at all.

We were all very relieved.

After that we went home and performed the whole play all over again for Tilly and Noah and Mum, this time with less talc. (We kept in the rolling donkey head, though; Joel insisted.)

That weekend I put the Hogwarty Shakespeare book back on the shelf in Mum's office, and spent all Saturday night curled up with Mum and Joel, watching Ekaterina Yashvilinova DVDs. (Joel fell asleep.)

Sunday was Easter Sunday.

'It's chocolate day!' yelled Noah, running in through the front door with his mouth all smeary.

'We had chocolate for breakfast!' yelled Tilly, running in after him.

'As you can possibly tell,' said Bridget, sighing as she carried in their bags after their overnight stay.

'I haven't started mine yet,' said Jem smugly, carrying a large gold-foil-wrapped chocolate egg in her arms.

'Me neither,' I said.

We'd made a pact beforehand: no chocolate eating till she was back. Which was probably a bit easier for me, since Mum wouldn't let us have our eggs till after Sunday lunch anyway. We were having roast chicken with all the trimmings. I'd spent ages laying the table in the kitchen – with a long white cloth, and candles, and little name cards in fancy curly writing, with chicks and ducks drawn on them. I'd put on my best dress too: a dark blue velvet one with a bow that tied at the back. I had brushed out my hair and pushed it back with a silver band.

'Oh, Georgie! Don't you look a picture. Give me a hug, beautiful girl,' said Bridget, squeezing me tightly.

No one else was dressed up. Bridget was wearing a saggy grey dress with a hole in the pocket, lots of purple eyeliner, and dangly earrings with huge dragons on them. Jem had her wonky patchwork skirt on. The others were all in jeans and tops. Not that long ago it would've made me feel silly. I would've gone upstairs to change, and come down with my face all red. But I didn't mind things like that so much any more. I wasn't dressing up for anyone but me. So if I liked it, that was all that mattered.

'Somebody want to give me a hand with potatoes?' said Joel, waving a knife.

We all did some kitchen things. Then me and Jem took Tilly and Noah out to Queen's Park to run off some of their chocolate energy before we risked giving them any more.

When we got back, there was hot roast chicken on the table.

'Allowed to treat ourselves every now and then, aren't we?' said Mina, frowning as she added four roast potatoes to her plate.

'Yes!' said everyone.

'This is yummy,' said Tilly, with her mouth full.

'Even though it's not even chocolate,' said Noah, having seconds.

After lunch we waved Bridget off back to Croydon, and made a new pact to ignore all the washing-up till later.

'Can we have more eggs now?' asked Tilly, cramming the last of the one from her mum into her mouth.

'Oi!' said Joel, giving her a prod. 'You're supposed to wait to be given a gift, not go sticking your hand out. Although – I suppose, if you really wanted them, you'd go looking . . .'

'Ooh! Are we having an egg hunt?' asked Jem. 'We used to do that in our old flat, but it was rubbish because there were only about three places to hide anything. This is going to take for ever!'

I looked at Mum. 'Yes, you too, silly,' she said. 'Go on. No taking ones that don't have your name on, please!'

I had an egg from Mum and Joel hidden under my bed; one from Bridget that was in Tilly's shoebox doll's house; a bag of mini jelly eggs that Granny had sent dangling from a windowsill; and a card from my aunts with a cheque inside.

The others all had little piles of different-sized eggs too.

'I'm drinking my coffee, darlings,' said Mum, looking confused as Tilly led everyone to the little back room with the knobbly sofas.

'Nope,' said Tilly. '*We're* deciding what happens now, and this is what we decided, and you'll see very soon because it is a surprise.'

'We have some things for you too,' I said, feeling quite shy again all of a sudden.

I looked at Jem. She was looking unusually shy – and nervous too.

'I spent ages thinking of what spell I could make – especially for you, Mina, because I know you don't really like having loads of chocolate in the house, and I thought maybe I could make it so that you liked it after all. But actually I have an announcement to make. I'm giving up being a witch.'

Tilly and Noah gasped.

'It isn't because I'm *not* one. But I think sometimes I try too hard to fix things, when actually I could just get on with being myself. So that's my Easter present.'

'You can't eat that,' whispered Noah.

Tilly sighed.

'I think it's a grand present,' said Joel. 'Now – Georgie, did you want to go next?'

I felt very shy then. But I reached into my bag, which was tucked behind the sofa, and pulled out a small squashy parcel wrapped in lilac tissue paper.

Mum sat up, her lips parting with surprise. 'For me? Oh . . .'

She carefully unwrapped the parcel, folding back the tissue till it was revealed: a purple velvet egg cosy, shaped like a crown, with lots of gold braid and fake jewels sewn round the edges. It was completely imperfect. It would've been much better if Jem had sewn it. But I'd tried really hard.

'Did you make this yourself?'

'I had a lot of help.'

'Oh, Georgie, I love it!'

Then I reached into the bag and pulled out a lilac-tissue parcel for Joel too. Joel's egg cosy was also purple, but with silver thread.

'Well, aren't you clever,' said Mum, giving me a squeeze.

Tilly and Noah whispered furtively between themselves. Then Tilly coughed.

'Excuse me, but there is another Easter sort of present to happen, and it is for everyone, but especially Mina, and we have to turn out all the lights now, so shush.'

The room was suddenly plunged into darkness.

'What are they doing?' I hissed.

'Not a clue,' Jem hissed back.

There was a lot of rustling and muttering.

Then the lights flicked back on.

On the coffee table in the middle of the room sat an ostrich egg.

Well, sort of. It was about the same size as the old one from the mantelpiece, but this one was covered in cracks, as if it had been broken and then pieced back together again. The gaps in between were gold and shiny, as if metal was binding it all together.

'Oh!' said Mum, covering her mouth with her hands.

'It isn't real gold,' explained Tilly. 'But it is the real egg.'

'I'm very sorry,' said Noah. 'I broke it. And I pretended I didn't because it made you sad. And then we tried to buy a new one.'

'I started my own business,' said Tilly. 'Lots of them. I'm nearly as famous as you at school now.'

'And I sold all the Morrises,' said Noah.

'Oh, Nono!' I said.

No wonder he'd been hugging the cushions.

'It's OK. I'm over it now.' He sniffed and wiped away a tear. 'But when we went back on eBay, the egg we were going to buy was sold already.'

Tilly nodded. 'At school we did this project thing about Japan, and about how if they break a precious bowl there, they use molten gold to glue it all back together, and it makes something new and beautiful and precious all over again. We couldn't afford any molten gold though.'

'Sorry. It's just a balloon.'

'But we did make something new and beautiful and precious. We think so, anyway. We hope you like it.'

Tilly did a little curtsy. Noah did one too.

Then Mum burst out into a huge sob. 'Oh, I love it – come here!' She wrapped them in her arms and cried into their hair.

'I think she liked it OK,' said Joel, grinning.

We all carefully picked up the egg and passed it around. It was very light, and very delicate, and somehow even more special than it had ever been before.

A superglue egg for our superglue family.

Mum placed it very carefully back on the stand on the mantelpiece.

Then they all went off to find some tissues, and more coffee.

Jem and I lay down on the floor on the rug, like before, staring up at the egg in wonder.

'It's so cool,' whispered Jem.

'It is. It really is. Like magic. Only – not. Better.'

'I can't believe no one gave her any actual chocolate though,' whispered Jem.

'Me neither!'

'I mean . . . if I'd lost a precious ostrich egg, I'd be glad to have it back. But . . .'

'And if someone had made me a lovely egg cosy, all with their own hands, that would be nice too. But . . .'

So we both put one of our eggs on the mantelpiece too, next to the ostrich one, for sharing.

And THEN they all lived happily ever after.

We still haven't yet, Jem.

We are, though. We're doing it right now.

Yes. Yes, we are.

If you've enjoyed reading about Georgie and Jem, you'll love Susie's other books about Pea Llewellyn.

Turn the page for a little taste.

HAPPY READING!

CHAPTER 1

GOODBYE

'There,' said Pea, propping up her creation on the mantelpiece. 'Told you I'd have time to finish it.'

She stepped back and considered her handiwork. It was a blue plaque – the sort they put outside houses where famous writers once lived, to make people say 'Oh!' and fall off the pavement. This one was more of a blue plate, really. The writing was in silver marker that was running out. She'd spelled *Author* wrong due to the pressure of the moment – but it would do till there was a real one.

'It's *nice*,' said Clover doubtfully, peering over

the top of Pea's head. 'But why isn't my name on it?'

'Mine isn't either,' said Pea. 'Or Tinkerbell's, though I suppose I could add us. Somewhere.'

'Don't bother with mine,' said Tinkerbell, clicking one end of a pair of handcuffs closed around her tiny wrist. '*I'm* not going anywhere.'

With a click, the other cuff snapped shut around the fat wooden leg of the sofa.

With a gulp, the key disappeared down Wuffly the dog.

It was the day the Llewellyn sisters were to leave the sleepy seaside town of Tenby for their new life in London. So far, it was not going exactly as planned. The electricity had been cut off a day too soon. Tinkerbell's father Clem (who had stayed overnight just to keep an eye on things, as he often did lately) had made a bonfire in the front yard to cook toast over, stuck on the end of a twig, and accidentally set fire to the front door. The removal van had arrived three hours early, and left without warning, taking with it breakfast, their hairbrushes, and all but one of Clover's shoes.

But not, apparently, a pair of handcuffs.

Pea was secretly pleased. Clem had put out the fire before she could dial 999, but now they had an excuse. Perhaps she could locate a kitten for the firefighters to rescue too, while they were in the area. In gratitude, they might offer to take them by fire engine all the way to London, sirens on. That would be the ideal introduction to city life.

City life was something of a mystery to Pea, but she couldn't wait to meet it. She'd made everyone play Monopoly after tea for weeks, for research. London seemed to be mostly about rent and tax, going to jail, and being a top hat. Old Kent Road was brown. According to films, there were also red buses, Victorian pickpockets, and all houses had a view of Big Ben. It was going to be brilliant.

'*Please* tell me you've got a spare key for those cuffs,' said Clem as he chased Wuffly around the ancient blue sofa.

'There's a car coming!' cried Clover, wobbling on one shoe.

Tinkerbell sat on the floorboards, cross-legged, drawing a picture of a mermaid with perfect concentration.

Wuffly made a break for the open door of the flat.

Clem gave chase.

The blue plate toppled off the mantelpiece with a smash.

Pea knelt beside the pieces, and clutched her thumbs tightly in her fists. She'd seen it on a poster in the library. It was supposed to stop you from crying – something about redirecting the electricity inside your brain. It never worked.

'Oh, don't, please don't! We can fix it!' said Clover, who hated anyone getting teary (despite being quite the expert herself), especially on important days. But the glue was in a box on its way to London. So were all the other blue plates.

'Well, we'll make another one when we

arrive. A brand-new one for our brand-new house.'

'But it isn't *for* the new house,' Pea said. The new house hadn't earned a blue plaque yet. It was for *this* house, like a goodbye present. But that was the sort of thing Clover wouldn't understand, like saving the nuttiest square of chocolate for last.

Clover eyed Tinkerbell. 'Don't stress. At this rate, we might never get there.'

Pea looked at the plate jigsaw (wondering half-heartedly if the firefighters might be able to fix it), then looked at Tinkerbell, and sighed. As the eldest, Clover was supposed to be the mean one, really, but she'd never been very good at it.

'You can't stay here, Tink,' Pea said gently, taking her drawing pencil. 'Clem burned all the chairs. And you're too little to be left behind to look after yourself.'

'I'm *seven*, not five,' said Tinkerbell drily, producing a new pencil from her pocket.

'You won't even remember this place once

you see our new house,' said Pea, watching as Tinkerbell gave the mermaid horns and a tail. 'I expect it's more like a palace, really. With turrets, a drawbridge—'

'*Loads* of handsome princes,' said Clover.

'If you like.' Pea suspected Tinkerbell would be more interested in dungeons, but Clover was thirteen, and Pea had read all about hormones and mind-altering lip gloss. She herself intended to stay sensibly eleven for as long as possible.

'She's here!' shouted Clem from the stairs as Wuffly barked a mad fanfare.

Pea ran to join Clover at the first-floor window. With a scrape, and a bit of help with pulling the sofa, Tinkerbell followed. Even Wuffly reappeared, to press her wet nose against the glass.

It was a taxi. Not the usual Tenby sort, with DAVECABS and a phone number stickered to the door, but a proper black London cab with an orange lamp. And climbing out was no ordinary passenger.

It was Mum.

Bree Llewellyn, who had lived for the last four years in this tiny first-floor flat with her three girls, making ends meet while she typed, and typed, and hoped.

But Bree Llewellyn was no more. The birdlike blonde goddess stepping out of that taxi was now better known as Marina Cove – bestselling author of the *Mermaid Girls* books.

They waited for her to wave up at them, but there was a handful of girls on the doorstep, clutching books to be signed.

'She's so good with the fans,' breathed Clover.

Privately, Pea thought Clover sounded a bit daft when she repeated other grown-ups' words like that. But it was true: their mother always gave her readers plenty of attention. They watched her pose for photographs, and write her not-real name in the front of books, and Pea very quietly and privately missed the days when she had belonged just to them. Tinkerbell's mermaid, with the horns and tail, ended up on top of a thickly scribbled furniture bonfire, engulfed in red-pencil flames.

Then there were footsteps on the stairs, dainty and clicky.

There she was in the open doorway, great clouds of blonde hair flowing over her shoulders, long skirt shimmering like silver scales. Marina Cove, the famous writer.

'What *have* you done to our front door?' she said, folding her arms severely across her chest.

And then she was Mum again, and everything was all right.

Pea showed her the bits of blue plate, and felt herself wrapped up in a hug that seemed to put it back together again – all wool and hair, and the perfume-smell of jasmine flowers.

Clover limped over – the one shoe that had been left behind was a clog – and joined in, while Clem explained about the fire, and the chairs, and why no one had brushed their hair. (Not that anyone would've noticed. Clover resembled her mother exactly, including the ability to roll out of bed with hair all twirled and tousled as if it had been arranged that way on purpose. Tinkerbell took after her father, Clem, who was Jamaican by way of Birmingham, so her curls needed rebraiding tightly to her head once a week with a blob of CurlyGurl coconut goop to stop her from going fluffy. Only Pea required a regular morning taming, but on Clover's advice she was learning to describe her bright orange mane as 'Pre-Raphaelite' as opposed to 'ginger frizz'. In any case, it did the job of distracting from her chin, which was of a size people mention.)

'I did try,' said Clem, who was looking quite tired by now, and kept glancing hopefully at his watch.

'Oh, who cares about a few tangles,' said Mum. 'I've been looking forward to today for so long, my darlings, and I'm not going to let a single thing ruin it.'

Pea winced, and reluctantly stepped back so Mum could see Tinkerbell.

But Tinkerbell was sitting on the sofa, quite unhandcuffed, throwing a scrumpled ball of drawing paper for Wuffly to chase.

'There you are, pickle!' said Mum, sweeping her up into a great whirling hug of her own. 'Have you been awful for Daddy? I hope so.'

'Of course I had a spare key,' Tinkerbell hissed, once Mum had let her go and gone off to inspect the oddly naked kitchen. She dropped the key into Clem's hands, reluctantly followed by the cuffs. 'You won't tell, will you?'

Clem shook his head wearily.

It was time to go. Especially for Clem, whose job was showing empty houses to people like Mum who needed new ones, and who was supposed to have been unlocking 8 Harbour Court for a nice young couple from Saundersfoot an hour ago.

'See you soon then, girls,' he said, kissing

Mum's cheek. 'I'll come up to visit, check out your new digs once you're all settled, right?'

Marina lives with her three girls and a dog by the sea – that's what it said on the back page of the *Mermaid Girls* books. Clem hadn't lived with them for three years, and he was technically only Tinkerbell's dad. But he was still Pea's Clem – and Clover's, and always a little bit Mum's. Suddenly it felt quite wrong to be going off to all the exciting tax and jail and pickpockets without him.

'Weekly email with all your news, remember?' he whispered in Pea's ear when it was her turn for a goodbye hug.

'With bullet points,' she whispered back, holding on extra tight.

He thudded down the stairs at speed.

'Will he really come to visit?' asked Tinkerbell.

'Of course! We're moving to London, not Mars,' said Mum, tucking Tinkerbell's chin into the crook of her arm. 'Now come on, before that taxi driver thinks we've changed our minds.'

She hurried them out with their one remaining suitcase before anyone could stop for a last look and feel the tiniest bit sad.

'Goodbye, little flat!' she shouted as she tapped down the stairs.

'Goodbye, shower that never stays hot!' sang Clover.

'Goodbye, mouldy ceiling!' said Pea.

'Goodbye, home,' said Tinkerbell.

And they all piled into the black cab.

SUSIE DAY

The Secrets of Billie Bright
9780141375335

The Secrets of Sam and Sam
9780141375281

Pea's Book of Best Friends
9780141375328

Pea's Book of Big Dreams
9780141375311

Pea's Book of Birthdays
9780141375298

Pea's Book of Holidays
9780141375304

Warning! These books do not contain mermaids.